BLOOD FOR THE MARKED MAN

A NOVEL OF THE OVERNIGHT BY
DON KILCOYNE

Thanks to my friends at the New York Renaissance Faire (still the best entertainment value in history) especially Bethany Coslar, Stephen Brock and Lars Lunde, who know how to make work feel like play, and to my Bride and Joy, Kelly Kilcoyne.

This is a work of fiction. Any resemblance to actual persons living, dead or undead is purely coincidental.

Copyright © 2011 by Don Kilcoyne

All rights reserved. This book or any portion thereof may not be reproduced or used in any manner whatsoever without the express written permission of the publisher except for the use of brief quotations in a book review.

Printed in the United States of America

Second Printing, 2012

ISBN-13: 978-1477694961
ISBN-10: 147769496X

Kilcoyne Books
Warwick, NY 10990

donkilcoyne.com

1

The bar was dimly lit. And so was I.

It was a little after 8 PM. Knobs and I had been sipping on some 12-year-old single malts at The Rat Bastard for about four hours. The Red Sox were flaying the Yankees on four TVs. All the Bastard regulars were already half in the bag: senior delinquent Jay "The Voice" Kaminski, chubby little accountant Solly Suk, Rat Bastard proprietor Michael "Wee Mickey" Sturgis, Phil LeBlanc, Chris Gannon and Tyrell "Phlegm" Williams. The only Rat missing was Anton "Cheeky" Chekowicz. We'd buried him that morning.

Jay and the rest of the Bastards were perched on their barstools, hovering around an extremely hot redhead, who had the poor fortune to be the only woman at the bar, like kids around a birthday cake. As a student of human nature, I figured Phil and Chris, two decently fit thirty-somethings, might actually have a shot at a looker like her, but it was Phlegm's long lanky frame that loomed over her like a busted patio umbrella. His face was flushed, his breathing tight. He had it bad for the girl.

Knobs raised his glass and said, "To the end of Cheeky's terrible, horrible, no good, very bad year."

We all raised our glasses. Knobs and I clinked. "Hear hear."

"To Cheeky Chekowicz," I added "— the vampire who wasn't a vampire."

"He had you thons of bitcheth fooled," said Phlegm Williams.

"Blow me," I cleverly retorted. "He looked like a vampire, thirsted like a vampire. He even scorched in the sun like a vampire. The back seat of my car still smells like bacon. If it looks like a duck…"

Knobs nodded, "Hell, even other vampires thought he was a vampire."

Phlegm cleared his throat and spit into a napkin. We all reflexively looked away. "Ever figure out what the fuck he really wath?"

I sipped my scotch. The real story was uber-confidential, but hey, we were among friends who wouldn't understand a word of it anyway. "Yeah, funny story about that: it turns out some Babylonian she-demon whatsis had pumped and dumped him as part of her plan to ignite a vampire-mortal race war."

"So it was an honest mistake on your part?" asked Chris.

"Yep. Just an honest mistake. No harm done."

No, Cheeky had been no nightwalker, no Nosferatu, no Wampyr. Just a sad little guy that nobody'd ever liked, who'd died of a cancer that nobody ever walked for, and got buried after a funeral that none of these Bastards even bothered to show up for.

Knobs and I had arranged for a simple grave side ceremony: a bible verse or two, a few respectful words from a local minister. A close friend, Rev. Mossier, did the honors, then invited Knobs and I to add any thoughts on Cheeky's life. I passed. Knobs just muttered, "Stay dead, ya little bastard." He'd meant it affectionately.

I pictured the cemetery men lowering the casket with Cheeky's body into the large grave, then the box with his head into the smaller hole a few feet away, and wondered if separating the head had been absolutely necessary. Better safe, right? Cheeky had been an unpredictable little prick the last year of his life, so the two-coffin package had probably been a prudent investment. Wee Mickey even took up a collection at the Rat Bastard for a handsome little hand-carved hickory stake for his heart. "From the Bastard Boys." I think Cheeky would have appreciated the gesture.

I sipped my fourth Macallan and reflected privately to Knobs that I could tell some stories about the Cheek, but I was not the kind of man to speak ill of the dead—or the undead, for that matter. Then some jackass spoiled the misty moisty moment by opening his big beer-powered mouth.

"Goddamn freak turned into a vampire on that very stool!"

At the other end of the bar, Wee Mickey held the small audience enthralled with his hundred-some-oddth telling of his brush with fame. His disturbingly huge hands flailed like a carnival barker, occasionally pausing to push his black, mid-90s John Mellencamp mop off his wee face. There were only eight of us in the bar. Seven of us were regulars. So Mickey's yarn was for the benefit of the redhead sitting on the "very" stool the man was standing on tip-toes to point at. "Here's to Cheeky 'Can I Put That on the Tab I Never Fuckin' Pay' Chekowicz."

"Hey, watch your language, Mick," I protested. "The man is dead."

"For real this time?" Mickey turned his attention back to his audience. "You know what he did? Right here? Another round for everyone?" Six heads nodded. "He started puking up blood and shit and his own entrails. Entrails! Right..." He flicked his dingy yellow towel across the bar top at the hottie's blue jean-wrapped butt. Whack! "...on this bar stool." She squealed, caught the towel and gave it a tug, nearly pulling Wee Mickey right over the bar. "HO! Whoa! Let go!" he squeaked. She did. "Ha!" Mickey sounded a little shrill. A little too excited. "Where was I? Oh yeah. Entrails! Right on that chair! Don't you worry, Gina!" He gave a little mock swirl with the towel. "I wiped it down."

Anyone who'd spent more than 20 minutes at The Rat Bastard in the past six months had heard the infamous story of the vampire wannabe. Many a night Knobs and I had cheerfully chipped in our own gory details. As the arresting officers, we'd carried the puking, crapping little monster to our once-pristine squad car. Most nights you can get a few drinks bought for you with a story like that. But most nights I haven't just been to the man's funeral. Wee Mickey was working my nerves. And talk of entrails was pissing me off. I was there. No entrails had been involved.

"Mickey, not tonight."

"'C'mon, Angus! Lighten up! Tell Gina how ya made him hang his head out the squad car window all the way to the..."

"Stow it, Mick," said Knobs, eyes glued to the Yankees game on the TV over the bar. "Respect." Detective Darius Knobs is ten years my junior. We've worked like partners for almost a dozen years. He's a big guy, 6-foot-5, 225, with broad, thick shoulders and forearms like fence posts. Nine out of ten times, when Knobs says "Stow it," it gets stowed.

"Who the fuck you two Nazis think you are?"

All conversation stopped. Jay "The Voice" Kaminski had just said something profoundly stupid.

We call Jay "The Voice" because he's the singular dominant sound in the Rat Bastard. Louder than the Wurlitzer, harsher than the Osterizer, Jay's voice is a bellowing, scratchy chain saw that's usually saying something stupid and never, ever shuts up. No matter what game's on, Jay raucously roots against the home team. When a politician gets caught with his pants down, literally, figuratively or both, Jay will insist, non-stop, at the top of his lungs, that it took balls. "BALLS!" he'll tell you, over and over again, "BALLS!" Jay's a vocal majority of one. He dramatically buys the first round when no one's at the bar yet, he's always right, and he never leaves before last call. When he does leave, it's usually on his Harley, which he drives, white knuckled and sweating, at about 20 miles an hour. I don't know how he keeps it vertical.

The vocal chain saw fired up again. "Who the fuck you think you are, tellin' us what we can talk about in our own bar?"

"You know who I am, Jay," I said. "And you've heard this story a hundred times. So just watch the game, and shut up, OK?"

"Fuck you, Wellstone. You're not on duty. This is still fuckin' America and if Mickey wants to tell a story no fascist cop is gonna stop him. And Gina here," he paused and literally licked his lips after saying her name. "hasn't heard the story. Tell the story, Mickey."

It takes a special kind of stupid to pick a fight with a cop. Especially a cop you've known personally for thirty years, who's been drinking for four hours with his 225-pound best friend at his side. A very, very special stupid. And, as much as I wanted to bust Jay in the mouth, something kept nagging at me: Jay, on his worst day, was just run-of-the-mill stupid. He wasn't usually THIS kind of stupid. So what the hell was going on?

"Fuck Wellstone, Mickey," he bellowed. "Finish the story!"

"Nah, Jay," said Mickey, distractedly rinsing and re-rinsing pilsner glasses. "I think Angus is right. It's not respectful. I'll tell it tomorrow."

"Tell it now! Gina wants to hear it." He licked his lips again. Gross. "Don't you, sweetheart?"

Gina hesitated, looked around at the seven men in the room. Her eyes lingered on Knobs an uncomfortably long time. He didn't notice. "No, I'm good, Jay. If Captain America here says enough, then I've heard enough. I get the gist."

Jay's jaw dropped. His gazed traced the electric line between Gina's eyes and Knobs' sledge-hammer chin. He glared at Gina and slammed his Yankees cap on the bar. "No you don't! What the fuck is with you people? Cheeky was a cheap, backstabbing, tip-stealing weasel who wouldn't stand his round if he hit the goddamned lottery! And you're acting like you buried Mahatma fuckin' Ali! He's dead! He should have died six months ago with a stake through his heart before he got your wife kidnapped," he jabbed his cap at me, then at Knobs "and your girlfriend turned into some wolf bitch."

At "girlfriend" he turned to sneer at Gina. (What is this, I thought, sixth grade?) At "wolf bitch" he backhanded Knobs across the chest with the Yankees cap.

Knobs didn't even look up. He caught Jay's wrist and squeezed. Snatch. Crunch. "AAAGGGH!" With his other hand, he grabbed the offending cap and tossed it into the back bar trash, where it sank into a pile of half-eaten nachos, wings and blue-cheese dressing. Jay choked out something about the cap being a "World Series collector's" something or other. Knobs took a sip of his scotch. His gaze never left the TV.

Here's something you should know about Knobs. A rugby player since high school, and Special Forces after college, Knobs is easily the scariest hand-to-hand ass-kicking motherfucker I've ever met. He's earned belts in colors Martha Stewart hasn't heard of, in disciplines I can't even pronounce. He's got three scars down each thigh as souvenirs of the night he single-handedly punched a werewolf to death. Jay taking on Knobs was like a double-wide trailer yelling "bring it!" at a tornado. Jay knew all of that, and picked a fight anyway.

"Oh, Jesus Christ motherfucking shitfucker goddamn hand you're breaking my fucking..."

While Jay screams, let's take a moment to clear one thing up. Jay was right about Cheeky. 100 percent. Cheeky was an absolute parasite. A screw up. A danger to himself and a burden on the community. His fuck-ups had almost gotten my wife killed. He'd gotten Knobs' fiancée, Shelly, mauled and turned into a lycanthrope. He'd wrecked my car and I spent an evening in Kazakhstan freezing my ass off discussing quantum theology with the Baba Yaga. All because of Anton Chekowicz. I hated the little son of a bitch. But after everything that Cheeky had put Knobs and I through together, we thought of Cheeky as our son of a bitch, and ours alone. If anybody was going to speak ill of this particular dead guy, it was going to be us. We'd earned it.

Jay, his wrist still clamped in an iron grip, ran out of obscenities and just started spurting vowels as Knobs watched the game and Gina watched Knobs. The scarlet beauty shifted in her seat seductively and whispered something to Phlegm Williams.

"You think tho?" Phlegm asked doubtfully, speckles of spit catching in the corner of his mouth. She brushed her fingertips along the back of his bony hand and nodded once. Phlegm poked Chris Gannon in the shoulder and gestured at Knobs. Gannon's eyes flew open like garage doors as he shook his head no. Phlegm looked back at Gina. She nodded "yes" and stroked his hand again. Phlegm grabbed Gannon's arm and shoved him toward Knobs, who appeared oblivious to the whole thing. Jay just kept blubbering for Knobs to release his wrist.

Gannon tried to backpedal away from Knobs just as Gina rose from her stool. The two collided. Gina steadied herself by grabbing Gannon's right arm—the one he calls Gannon's Cannon. Gina cooed and squeezed the bicep like she'd never touched a grown man before. She batted her eyes at Gannon and nodded, tilting her head toward Knobs in clear invitation to combat. Solly, a tiny middle-aged accountant in a Rat Bastard softball jersey, saw which way the wind was blowing and tried to intercept his friends. "Hey, listen, no harm done. Wow, bad luck about the hat. Get another one on eBay, get that wrist checked out and why don't we ALL go to the hospital…" but Gina released Gannon and he shot toward Knobs, mowing Solly over like a stalk of wheat.

I just shook my head. I shoved myself away from the bar and dropped, a little unsteadily, to my feet, ready for anything, I hoped. I started to warn Chris off, but my scotch-soggy tongue wouldn't move with its usual alacrity. By the time I spit out "don't," they'd already begun.

Knobs released Jay, swung around and pushed me back down onto my stool. "I got this one," he said, as Gannon plummeted forward, swinging a haymaker at Knobs' head. With one smooth motion, Knobs threw his right elbow, blocking Gannon's punch with a nauseating crunch of finger bones and followed through to meet Gannon's head with a meaty forearm. Gannon's eyes rolled back in his head as he collapsed.

As Gannon dropped, Phil LeBlanc turned heel and headed for the door. Gina was having none of that. She whispered urgently to Phlegm, who grabbed Phil by the coat and shoved him back toward the bar. Gina stepped directly into Phil's path. He caromed off her like he'd hit a stone column. Gina stood her ground, catching Phil by the shoulders, caressed his face and whispered something that I couldn't quite hear. Phil growled deep in his chest and reached for Knobs. Still on his barstool, Knobs put his size twelve Timberland on Phil's chest and shoved him back across the room, over a table and onto the floor. By now all the men in the bar, with the exception of Knobs and myself, were puffing like bulls in heat. Even Mickey, cowering behind the bar, looked like he'd just done an eightball of coke. Something was definitely wrong with these guys.

Jay, still whining about his battered wrist, held it out for Gina's sympathy. She cupped it in her palm and gently kissed his pulse-point. From the look on his face you'd think she was giving him head. When she released him, he roared like a silverback gorilla, grabbed a beer bottle and swung with all his might at the back of Knobs' skull. I staggered between them and managed to catch Jay's arm, but I had to throw all my weight on it—ultimately fracturing it across the edge of the bar—to get him to let go of the bottle.

Knobs finally stood up. He took two steps toward Phlegm then spun and punched Gina square in the mouth. I heard bones crack as Knobs' huge right fist drove her lower jaw deep into her throat. Her eyes glazed, blood spurted like a burst pipe and she collapsed on the barroom floor.

"Jesus Christ!" I screamed like a little girl. Everyone else froze. Knobs sat back down, sipped his beer and stared up at the Yankees' game. 6-0, Sox. 8th inning. I grabbed a handful of bar rags and ran to Gina, whose strawberry hair was soaking in a puddle of crimson blood.

"Leave 'er," said Knobs.

"Yeah, can't do that, pal. What the fuck?"

"She'll be OK, Angus. Leave her. Mick?" said Knobs as I started dialing 911 for an ambulance. "Did you hire her or is she freelance?"

"Who? What are you talkin' about?"

"Who, Mickey? Really? Her who." Knobs gently nudged Gina with his foot. She groaned.

"Wha... Gina? Hire her for what?"

"Mickey, answer the fuckin' question. It's not against the law... yet. Is the succubus freelance or an employee?"

"Goddamnit." Mickey threw me a fresh towel. "Angus, please don't call anyone. Really, she'll be OK." Gina groaned again and started to sit up. Hooking her fingers over her lower teeth, she pulled her jaw back into position with a gurgle like flesh being dragged over wet gravel.

"Fug oo, Miggey," Gina spat, and shot him the bird to reiterate.

"Gina's a... freelance!"

"Fug oo! Agggh!" She wrestled with her jaw, re-seating it

properly. "Fuck. Fuck. You. Mickey. You hired me this afternoon then fucking pussied out like I knew you would!"

"I'm sorry, wait, what? The hell?" I had no idea what they were talking about.

"She's a succubus, Angus."

"Yeah, Knobs, I got that. Hired her for what?"

"Tell him, Mick."

"To spice the place up."

"This shithole?"

"Hey!"

"I mean, c'mon. You get chicks in here. Sometimes. Why are you paying to have chicks hang out in your bar? Wait, she's not a hooker, is she? 'Cause yeah, that's still a crime."

"I am not a hooker," said Gina, wiping the blood from her jaw and touching up her lipstick. "I am an ambient asset."

No clue, and my face couldn't hide it.

"My pheromones promote the production of testosterone. The more testosterone in a room, the more competitive guys get. They drink more. They step it up with the ladies, buying expensive cocktails instead of pitchers of Budweiser. You know. Martini thingies. With flavors. More testosterone, more successful pickups. More people go home, get laid, remember what a great night they had at The Rat Bastard. They come back and bring friends. All because of the ambience. The hot sexy ambience. Me."

"You can do that…" I gestured broadly, taking in the overturned furniture, Gannon's unconscious body, Jay's wrist, "whenever you want? Why aren't you working for the Marines or something?"

Gina stepped over Gannon to get closer to the back-bar mirror. As she touched up her makeup she said, "I had to really crank it up to make that happen. And really it only works on losers."

"Screw you!" whined Jay.

"Don't think so, loser. When was the last time any of you got laid? I mean, c'mon. Detective Jawline here" Knobs, of course, "barely noticed I was in the room. And you…" she looked at me like a lab specimen, "kept checking out my ass but never reacted to the pheromones."

I confess she had a spectacular ass. But so does my bride Tami. And in general, when someone asks "When was the last time you got laid?" I'm more likely to consult my watch than my calendar. Not bragging. Just saying. In general, I married up on the Kelvin scale.

"So what's your story?" Gina pressed, squinting as if to read the fine print on my forehead or something. "Gay?"

"Nope. Just happy. Finish your story."

"Keep your eyes off my ass?"

"Not gonna guarantee that."

"Good. OK, so I show up for work and Mickey here is all whiny: 'I don't know about this. What if someone finds out?' Now, I drove 90 miles to get here. From frickin Wappingers' Falls. I'm turning around? No sir. Mickey says 'How about I comp dinner and drinks and we'll see how the night goes?'"

"He stiffed you," said Knobs.

"Yes. He fucking stiffed me."

"I didn't…"

"You stiffed her, Mickey." Knobs had spoken. This time everyone listened. "What does he owe you?"

"Hundred bucks."

"Pay her." Knobs' eyes were back on the ballgame as he spoke.

Mickey started to protest. So did Jay and Chris. Knobs put up one finger and they all shut up.

Mickey pulled two fifties from his register. Put both on the table. Gina's hand shot out to grab them, but Knobs was faster. He snatched one fifty without looking, handed it back to Mickey and swirled his finger, signaling "another round for everybody. On Gina."

That's when my cell phone rang. It was my wife, Tami.

"It's Ertzbeth. They think she's dying. She wants to see to you, Angus."

2

My name is Angus Wellstone. I'm a cop. Six years ago, Knobs and I went looking for a child killer and caught a werewolf named Lars Gustafson. We didn't kill him. We didn't hand him over to the government. We called the newspapers and CNN. We put mythology under the microscope. We introduced superstition to science. And most of all, we applied the rule of law.

A lot of people questioned our motives. Still do. They called us parasites and scumbags, just out for our fifteen minutes and a fat movie deal. Well, I'm still a Detective in New Jersey with two car loans and a mortgage. So that worked out real well. Some called us crusaders out to blow the lid off a government conspiracy. I wish I could cop to that one, but we didn't even know there was a conspiracy until we were right in the middle of it. So, sadly, no. Truth is, our motives were pretty simple and they're written right on the side of our cars, where anyone can read them: Protect and Serve. Yeah, it's a little Hallmark Card-y, but it's simple, it's honest and it keeps our priorities straight.

At the time, it never even occurred to me that burying a truth as big as "werewolf-at-large" might protect anyone who actually deserved protection. Instead, it seemed pretty clear that doing so would only protect dangerous secrets and serve the people who traded in them.

That's not my job. My job is to make sure that child killers like Gustafson, supernatural lycanthropic nightmare or not, stand trial like the criminals they are, and go to jail. Gustafson went to jail. I did my job.

Now, as a species, we do stupid things sometimes. But that doesn't mean we're stupid all the time. So it didn't take the world long to figure out that if there's one werewolf, there are probably dozens. Hundreds. Thousands. And if werewolves, why not vampires? Banshees? Leprechauns? (Note: To my knowledge, no one has yet reported a leprechaun sighting while sober.)

So in the best tradition of human understanding and peaceful pursuit of science, mankind declared war on the dead. Looking back, we call that period The Frenzy. First came the great Purge. Thousands died "the true death" on both sides. Worldwide, 'we' burned villages and plowed under thousands of ancient graveyards. We staked corpses and burned dogs alive. Then came the Reckonings. 'They' kidnapped children, and converted them to wampyr, wolf or worse.

'We.'

'They.'

For two years, the world went totally batshit.

Cities worldwide were locked down after dark. Martial law was in effect in the U.S. for nearly six months. Weeks-long shadow insurgencies raged in a dozen cities around the globe. No one slept at night. No one. The whole world existed at the frayed end of its own last nerve. That included my hometown, Hawthorne, New Jersey, where it had all begun. My little burg saw as much action as the old haunted cities like Paris, Istanbul, Calcutta, St. Petersburg and New Orleans. Bodies turned up on doorsteps every morning. Churches caught fire every week. The local cemetery was an armed camp. Our emergency services and PD were stretched way, way the hell past breaking.

Toward the end, we all worked double shifts for nearly two months. I lost twenty pounds. Knobs, thirty. Tami shepherded an emergency farmers' food bank during the brightest daylight hours while Knobs' new girlfriend, Dr. Michelle "Shelly" Johnson, took charge of the corpse disposal team. We were sleeping about four hours a day, working 19 and 20. Friends were dying. Worse, friends were killing.

I'd walk around my town during the day and, aside from the boarded up windows, it looked almost normal. Then I'd stumble upon a body in a doorway with his throat ripped open or her chest caved in with a stake. Or I'd find an open pit in the park with a child's charred remains. Every time, I'd whisper a quiet prayer that I wouldn't know this one. But I know a lot of people. Bodies turned up two or three times a week. We were under martial law; we could have buried the bodies and moved on, but we did our best to investigate each case. At least once a week we'd have to stop a mob from breaking into a private home because they suspected it might house a Nocturnal. Riot patrol in my own backyard. Let me tell you, that's not what I signed up for.

The night was, of course, worse. Every shadow held a threat. The "music of the night" was a symphony of screams, sirens, shotguns and sobbing.

I'll never forget the night they surrendered. It was just when I thought things couldn't get any worse. A cold fog had settled over most of the East coast. Perfect cover for mayhem. We were braced for anything. Then I got a call, at home, just at twilight, from an anonymous woman. She said I'd better lock myself and my family inside because something was coming. Something bad. I replied, "No shit. Where've you been the last two year?" She insisted it was worse than anything we'd been dealing with. And it was coming specifically for us. I didn't know if she was threatening or warning us, but that didn't really matter. I believed her. Tami, Shelly, Knobs and I boarded up, locked and loaded, inside the three bedroom 2 and a half bath Fortress Wellstone, and waited for all hell—more hell, that is—to break loose. We sat up all night, the only noise in the house the constant drone of CNN. That's who brought us the news of the armistice.

The Nightwalkers wanted to call it quits. We watched as leaders of their side stepped forward out of the fog at U.N. Plaza and offered a truce. They wanted to finally come in from the cold and make their peace with humanity. We could hardly deny them. We were exhausted. And they were led by Thomas Jefferson.

The order went around the world like wildfire: Stand down. Both sides. Stand down.

We emerged at dawn to find a new world. A world where someone finally had the guts to stop fighting.

I figured whatever had been coming "for us" had heard the stand-down order, too.

It took our respective leaders another two years to completely hammer out the international Twilight Statutes. I helped, somewhat. Mostly as a rallying figure for both sides, I guess. That's where I met Ertzbeth. Ertzbeth Bathory the Blood Countess. She was a delegate to the Twilight Conference. An elder of the Wampyr. And the most terrifyingly exquisite woman I've ever known.

What happened in Hawthorne six years ago changed the world. What fascinates me is how much it didn't change. Now we know that vampires and werewolves and things we can't even name really do walk the night. But is that change? They always had. Only now, they walk the aisles of Wal-Mart, too. And again, they always had. We just hadn't known what to look for. Their kids now go to school. That's big. Most of them had, of necessity, home schooled. They've all got civil rights. And obligations. They can't hunt us and we can't hunt them. (Of course, if it were that easy I'd happily hang up my gun and sword.) They drink regulated blood. Pay taxes. And vote. Openly. As an interest group.

And as a weird little side-effect, my formerly sleepy New Jersey town has turned into a modern Montgomery, Alabama and Haight Ashbury all rolled into one. It's become a symbol of the latest civil rights movement. Hawthorne now has the highest number of Nocturnals per capita of any U.S. city. Including Vegas. A lot of folks who embrace the reconciliation make Hawthorne a pilgrimage. Those who don't want peace make it a target. And just like Haight Ashbury, sooner or later all the freaks show up here. That's why the Co-Director of the U.S. Bureau of Nocturnal Affairs—a Cabinet-level position no less—sips absinthe in my living room and lets me in on everything. Sometimes I think he tells me stuff he won't tell the President. I don't blame him. Chances are, any blip on his radar will soon show up in handcuffs in my lockup.

So here's a measure of how weird our world has become: A beautiful ancient monster, who slaughtered virgins in a dungeon four hundred years ago, lay dying in a hospital in New York City. That's not the strange part. The thought of her lying there, suffering, was tearing this old, happily married cop's heart out.

3

On the way to the hospital, a young New York homicide detective named Griffin briefed us while we downed a thermos of scalding coffee.

"Ertzbeth Bathory," he began, reading from a dossier, "known as the Blood Countess, was the first of the European vampires to publicly out herself. She..."

I waved him off. "I wrote that dossier."

As I said, I had met Ertzbeth while working on the Twilight Statutes. For months I worked alongside this beautiful foreign creature. Her hair was dark honey. Her eyes were almost feline, with oblong pupils and deep brown irises with tiny golden flecks. Her eyelashes long and thick. She never wore makeup, but her lips were always flushed like she'd just pulled away from a deep kiss. She cultivated an Eastern European accent, complete with a teeth-licking lisp. She flirted with me out of habit. I adore my wife, Tami, and so does Ertzbeth. Ertzbeth calls my wife "The astonishing Thami" Since neither of us could possibly consider hurting "Thami," I ignored 'Beth's flirting. (To the best of my ability, that is—I'm noble, not feeble.) After one particularly long night of work, Ertzbeth opened a two-hundred-year-old bottle of Cognac, sank onto the couch in my living room and told Tami and me her story.

The Hungarian Countess Ertzbeth Bathory was vampirized as an innocent young virgin in 1576 in the woods outside the Castle Csejthe. While her sire and every other vampire in Eastern Europe haunted graveyards and ruins, scampering in the dark like giant ticks, Ertzbeth reveled in her youthful immortal beauty. She took countless village virgins as lovers, then drained their veins into giant golden bowls and bathed in their blood. For forty years peasants sent their daughters to die in Castle Csejthe. Finally—Ertzbeth doesn't know why and history is silent on the subject—the peasants found the courage to stop Ertzbeth's blood orgy.

They stormed the castle, as peasants will, and killed her mortal advisors. But they didn't kill her. They could have easily driven a stake through her heart if they'd had the heart themselves. But they didn't. Ertzbeth told us that a dozen men, swords dripping with the blood and gore of her court, surrounded by steaming corpses, simply stopped when they laid eyes on her. They'd fallen in love. That was the night Ertzbeth came into her real power.

Rather than fight her way out of the castle, only to live like one of the crypt crawlers she despised, she surrendered. Instead of killing her, the townspeople respectfully, almost gently, walled her into her own tower.

And still, they brought her tribute. Freshly killed lambs, their necks broken so they wouldn't spill any blood. Or birds, caught by falcons trained to drop their still-twitching prey on her windowsill. Someone even brought her the occasional flask of human blood. They brought books and read to her through the walls. Philosophy. Mathematics. Astronomy. A priest once read to her from the Bible. Once. Her screams drove him mad.

She survived in her family castle for decades.

Then one day she just left. She completely disappeared from history.

Four hundred years later she walked out to the center of United Nations Plaza with Thomas Jefferson, Lord Ruthven, the Baba Yaga and others, and surrendered all over again.

⋅ ⋅ ⋅ ⋅ ⋅

We got to Ertzbeth's room at St Vincent's around 2 AM. Someone had removed a crucifix from the wall over her bed. The clean white "t" it left behind testified that St. Vincent's was a Catholic hospital. A superfluous EKG sat silently on its cart, pushed out of the way against the wall. Two pints of whole blood hung from a pole by her shoulder. One was attached to an IV. The other was a feeding tube. I traced its path from the blood bag, up across her shoulder, under her chin and between her teeth. I coughed up bile and forced myself to swallow it back down. Her perfect lips were gone.

Griffin had tried to prepare us. He said she'd been pretty beaten up. She hadn't been beaten up. She'd been vivisected.

Her lips and her eyelids had been removed. Both ears. Both breasts. Both canine teeth—her fangs. The incisions—that's what they were, incisions—glistened like the fairy dust worn by little kids and Goth girls. I could see every wound because no one had dressed them. No point, really. Vampires don't bleed a lot, and they don't get infections. Ordinarily, an elder vampire like Ertzbeth would shake off wounds like these in a few hours. Given enough blood, she'd heal completely in a few days. That's what the IV and the feeding tube were for—to encourage her immortal body to begin regenerating. But the wounds weren't healing. In fact, they were festering. That's unheard of in a vampire.

I leaned over and kissed her cheek. "I'm so sorry, 'Beth. I'm here to help." I looked for some sign of awareness in her unlidded eyes. Nothing. No way to tell if she was awake or asleep, dead or... well, not quite dead.

"Hello, Detective Wellstone. Detective Knobs." A short, chubby man in scrubs and a lab coat put out his hand.

"Dr. Weintraub. I'm glad they called you in." Dr. Felix Weintraub had been the first doctor on the scene when we caught the werewolf, Gustafson, years ago. He'd been the first to realize what, exactly, we'd caught. And since that night, he'd made a specialty of Nocturnal biology. "What's happening here? Why is she... decaying... like this?"

"Whoever did the damage knew how to incapacitate a vampire. And he has a sadistic imagination. See this?" He opened a small specimen jar. Inside was a tiny patch of what looked like extremely fine steel wool. "I found this under her tongue. The lab says it's pure silver. Silver wool, if you will. Each and every wound is impregnated with hundreds of these fine silver fibers. That's why she's not healing."

I've seen vampires heal from injuries that would have killed Wile E. Coyote. If you don't pierce the heart or destroy the head, a Vampire can and will bounce back from just about any trauma. Garlic slows them down, holy water (if you really believe) can burn like acid, and religious totems (again, if you really, truly believe) will stop them in their tracks. But if you really want to ruin a vampire's night, use silver. Like lycanthropes, they're hopelessly allergic to it.

The psycho who attacked Ertzbeth had invented the Nocturnal equivalent of salt in a wound: every time he cut somewhere, he rubbed silver wool in. Thousand of fibers now peppered her torn flesh. They gave her wounds the strange glistening fairy dust effect I'd noticed walking in.

"What are you doing for her?" Knobs asked.

"I'm removing the fibers," said Weintraub.

"With what?"

He pulled a tiny pair of tweezers from his pocket. "This may take some time."

"She asked for me," I said. "Can she talk?"

"She talked to Lord B for nearly an hour, but she was in excruciating pain. We have her sedated. Absinthe. Lord B recommended it. It seems the Green Fairy can dull even a vampire's pain. It's the wormwood, I think. I'm certain she told B everything she knew before we put her out. I've been cleaning her wounds for about an hour. He's waiting for you in the chapel."

I kissed her forehead once again, this time with my eyes closed. My lips felt her cool, smooth skin while the eyes in my head saw her perfect face sleeping peacefully on my living room sofa. In my head I know she was once a monster. But that was so many lifetimes ago. This ruthlessly violated body was just my Ertzbeth. "'Beth. You know

I'm gonna get him. Nothing under the sun or moon will stop me." I turned toward the door before opening my eyes. As I walked out I think I heard her faint rasp, "I know."

• • • • •

I found Victor "Lord B" Ruthven in the chapel, as promised. He'd slung his traditional frock coat over the simple cross on the wall. Most folks think the Wampyr can't even look at a cross. Not true. A cross is only a symbol. It's the faith behind it that gives it power. Two pieces of wood nailed together in an empty room are simply two pieces of wood. Or a handy coat rack.

I offered B my hand. He took it and pulled me into a bear hug that nearly cracked my ribs. Then he grabbed my shoulders and planted a crisp dry kiss on each cheek. He repeated the ritual with Knobs.

In tight black slacks and an open-necked poet's shirt, B looked like he had stepped off the cover of a Harlequin romance. He dressed like a Goth because that's how he'd made his fortune. Before the Purges, you could find a "Lord B" shop in every upscale mall or arty neighborhood in America. Cashmere frock coats. Silk and linen poet shirts. Velvet "Westenra" dresses. Gaudy gold and platinum jewelry, in the shape of skulls, daggers, even crosses. No silver, though. Fancy that. You've seen the same crap in a thousand Hot Topics and Spencer's Gift shops all over the country. But Lord B's was extremely high quality crap. Solid gold. Real velvet. Imported silk. All of it starting at about my weekly take home pay. Included with each item was a hand-written verse from Lord B himself. It's no wonder most of his fans, including many of his friends, thought Victor Lord Ruthven was only a very shallow alias for George Gordon Noel, Lord Byron.

Business has never been better for the Lord B chain. From what I hear, nightwalkers of all types are very hot in popular music and TV. And since Lord B was the first period couturier to certify his designs as authentic, he's become the Alexander McQueen of the wealthy Wampyr-wannabe set.

But B wasn't there to sell me a shirt. The Lord B line had been entrusted to junior designers and business managers years ago. No, B was there in his official capacity as Co-Director of the Bureau of Nocturnal Affairs — the famous B.N.A. Together, he and my-favorite-ex-president James "Jimmy" Carter served as the chief law enforcement officers responsible for all cross-species crimes in the U.S.A. He'd been offered the job based on his work pushing through the peace treaty at the end of the Frenzy. Somehow he drove both sides to reach some real compromise and forge a lasting compact in the form of the Twilight Statutes. Even though he dined with (and sometimes on, I suppose) celebrities and world leaders, B never lost touch with the town that started it all.

"My friends, I need your help," he began. And he brought us up to speed.

4

Lord B briefed us on Ertzbeth's awful, terrifying day.

Ertzbeth resided in a Hell's Kitchen high-rise with her mortal lover, Peggy O'Farrel. Knobs and I had been there once before, during the Cheeky Chekowicz case. Dropped like a castle in between the tiny actor-infested West Side studio apartments and the luxury suites closer to Broadway, World Wide Plaza was probably the closest thing 'Beth could find to her ancestral home in Hungary. After being shut up in the same tower for forty years, maybe a tower was the only place she felt safe.

That afternoon, she had been taking her usual mid-day nap. Sometime between 3:30 and 4, someone got past armed guards in the lobby, around security cameras in the corridors, up a cam-equipped elevator and through her armored door.

Elder vampires are notoriously tough to sneak up on. You've seen those movies where the fearless vampire hunter creeps up to the coffin, stake raised, only to have the vampire wake up at the last moment and rip his throat out? Well that's pretty much what happens, so don't try it. The wampyr don't fall into comas during the day. They sleep. Just like us. And just like us, loud noises and noxious smells will wake them up. And there's the catch. Vampires can hear and smell like bloodhounds, so the sound of somebody tiptoeing around might not wake you up, but it would sound like an alarm clock—or a dinner gong—to them. Sound is one thing. Let's assume your kung fu is strong and you can creep in like a ninja. You'd better not get the least bit nervous—or have taken a piss or a crap since your last shower—because the stench of a drop of perspiration, a hint of urine or excrement—even halitosis—will yank a vampire from her sleep in seconds.

As if stalking an Elder wasn't improbable enough already, 'Beth's unearthly charisma makes hunting her nearly impossible. If a raging peasant mob of grieving parents couldn't resist her glamour, I wouldn't want to meet the bastard who could cut her down in cold blood. Scratch that. I did want to meet him, to return the favor.

B told us what 'Beth had told him:

Our cold-blooded bastard somehow worked his way to 'Beth's bedside. She woke to the agony of a two-inch hickory spike, soaked in garlic oil, piercing her left shoulder. The first thing she saw was a cordless nail gun, held in a long-fingered, rubber-gloved hand. As she reflexively began to sit up, her attacker shot another wooden nail into her chest an inch above her heart simply by bumping the nose of the gun against her. She sized up the situation in a fraction of a second.

She was naked. Her shoulder and breast were screaming in pain from the wood and poisonous garlic oil seeping into her system. A tall slim man in a military-style sweater and heavy rubber gloves was standing over her. A black balaclava hid most of his face. He held the nail gun in his right hand, pressed directly over her heart. She looked into his eyes, trying to measure him, to learn something more about his intentions. She saw nothing helpful. She nodded carefully and slowly lay back down.

The man in the mask flicked his gaze to the trigger of the nail gun. He did it again. He wanted her to look at it. She looked. His finger held the trigger completely depressed. Apparently this tool was one of the automatic models. Depressing the trigger charged the compressed gas; quickly bumping the nose against a firm surface fired a nail. No need to squeeze and reload. He was making it clear that any attempt to wrest the gun away would simply fire the deadly dart into her heart. She nodded.

With his left hand, he pulled a golf-ball-sized wad of silver fiber—the "silver wool" found under 'Beth's tongue—from a pouch on his belt. He wedged it tightly between the knuckles of his middle and ring fingers. He then drew a silver scalpel. He brandished the scalpel before her eyes twice, then thumped the nail gun against her breast twice. Message received: Pain or death. There was no hesitation: Elder vampires have overwhelming gifts of self-preservation. She'd endure the pain. She calculated that she was an incredibly fast healer and could afford to play for time. Sooner or later his attention would waver for a fraction of a second. That's all she'd need. And she'd be free. Then, she reasoned, she'd have plenty of time to leisurely empty the whole nail gun up his asshole.

Suddenly, with two quick strokes, he sliced her lips clean off. Ertzbeth told B that it was so fast she didn't even realize what he'd done until he'd pressed the silver wool into the wounds. As the pain drove her system into shock, he cut away her two long, sharp canine teeth. He shoved the silver into those wounds as well. Her whole body seized in a spasm. Every muscle cramped in agony. He casually stuck the tip of the scalpel into the flesh of her belly, wiped his gloved hand on her sheets, sat down on the edge of the bed and started asking questions. The nail gun never wavered.

He started with personal questions: "What does it feel like to drink blood from your own lover?" "Why didn't the mob kill you in 1572?"

She answered these questions calmly and as directly as she could, considering she was lisping through missing lips and teeth. "Where did you go when you finally left Castle Csejthe? Who hid you all those missing years?" These questions she wouldn't answer. Every time she hesitated, he cut. When she outright lied, he cut something off. He carefully arranged each piece on her belly like a tray of canapés.

"You helped throw Sir Francis Varney into Mount Vesuvius in 1846. Who helped you, and what did you do with his fortune?" Even in her brutalized condition, this came as a shock. According to B, the cabal who had finally put an end to "Varney the Vampire" had sworn each other to secrecy. He told me none of the surviving conspirators had mentioned it in over 150 years. Concluding that B had been one of the conspirators required absolutely none of my extensive detective training.

"She refused to say anything about Varney," said Lord B, "in spite of some extremely creative persuasion. Apparently that is why he finally lost control and did the damage you see in the room upstairs."

We silently chewed on that for a few seconds.

"Why did he finally let her go?" asked Knobs.

"Unfortunately, he did no such thing. Ertzbeth tells me he had given up questioning her, was tormenting her in a pure rage, and was prepared to the deliver the coup de grace when Peggy walked in and shot him."

"Shot him? Peggy? Good for her!" Knobs is not one for half-measures. Peggy, a tall, athletic redhead, lived with Ertzbeth as personal assistant, lover and occasional aperitif. Her wrists were usually wrapped in elegant silk bandages.

"She had been out for a run in the park. When she returned, she heard the commotion in Ertzbeth's room. She loaded a shotgun, kicked in the door and let him have it with both barrels."

"So where is he?" I asked.

"Dead?" Knobs suggested, hopefully.

"I am afraid not." B turned away and pulled his coat down from the cross. "He was wearing some kind of body armor. Not surprising for a mortal challenging one of the Wampyri."

"How do we know he's mortal?" I asked.

"He bleeds. The vest caught most of the shot, but apparently not all. Our technicians are separating the blood splatter patterns and should be able to tell us more about our intruder when they can isolate his blood."

"Isolate? From whose...?" Before Knobs could finish the question, we knew the answer.

"Peggy."

"Correct, Angus. She blasted him in the back, sent him tumbling across the bed. He dropped the nail gun. In agony, Ertzbeth began to rise. I must assume our sadist knew that, without the threat of a stake through the heart, The Blood Countess—even in her brutalized state—would destroy him easily. He had but one chance, and he took it. He raced across the room, just inches ahead of Ertzbeth, and sliced open Peggy's throat as he barreled past. He escaped through the apartment as Ertzbeth tried desperately to stop the bleeding."

"And...?"

"No."

"I'm so sorry..." Knobs instinctively made a tiny sign of the cross with his thumb. B winced slightly, and continued.

"We all are. But in dying, we believe Peggy may have saved her lover."

I protested, "Ertzbeth would never..."

"No! Of course not. No. I am sorry. Peggy's arterial spray drenched Ertzbeth's wounds. Think back to the ancient stories of the Blood Countess. They tell of her bathing in blood instead of drinking it. Dr. Weinberg theorizes her skin may be particularly porous and that she is capable of "drinking" blood by touch, consciously or no. She was desperately injured—even by Elder standards—and the silver in her wounds was corroding her flesh inch by inch. The blood she absorbed may have saved her from the true death."

"Poor Peggy." I had only met her a handful of times, but Peggy was a girl who made a lasting impression. Not only beautiful, which she certainly was, she was playful, clever and courageous. And I know that Ertzbeth loved her more than anything in the world. "B, I assume no one's mentioned Weinberg's theory to 'Beth."

"And I think it best we never do. Our dear friend has worked tirelessly for generations to make up for the suffering she caused in her early Blood Countess years. I think she would not consider the latest manifestation of her unique abilities a blessing. Peggy gave her life to save the woman she loves. Embellishments will not make her sacrifice any richer."

"I need to hit someone, soon, B," said Knobs. "Where do we start? You said you have some of the guy's blood?"

"Yes, I have had a sample sent to a Bureau lab near City Hall. We should hear something tomorrow morning—or should I say this morning? The sun is on the rise and I must get back to someplace more securely shaded. May I commandeer you a pair of beds? We shall all get some sleep and reconvene at dusk?"

I looked over at Knobs. His fists were clenched, the muscles in his forearms sticking out like hairy elevator cables.

"You know, B? I think we're going to get started on this. Your guys still at the apartment?"

"No, they have sealed it and gone back to the lab."

"Somebody there to let us in?"

"Of course. I'll call ahead and have someone open it up."

5

BNA crime scene investigators have access to everything from the latest forensics tech to the enhanced senses of vampires, lycanthropes—even ghouls if necessary. If the BNA had picked over Ertzbeth's apartment, I really didn't expect to stumble upon any case-breaking clues. But frankly, I didn't know where else to begin.

We started where our killer started—downstairs in the lobby. The doorman was a chatty old Nigerian gentleman, about five foot nothing, named Chukwuemeka Obgweh. "Call me Steve!" He had the brand of perfect diction that only proud recent immigrants seem to manage. He used an enthusiastic syntax, ending every sentence with a rising inflexion, like he was adding exclamation points in his head. His posture invested his gray hospitality uniform with the dignity of the military togs it was originally based on. In spite of the tragic business that had brought us to his door, speaking with him was delightfully rejuvenating.

"Steve, I'm sure you told the officers who were here today everything you saw, but now you've had a chance to think about it. To let it simmer a little. Did you notice anything at all strange about the visitors you allowed into the building today?"

"Yes, sir! No!"

"I'm sorry. Yes, or no?"

"Yes, sir, I told everything I know! No, I did not notice any strange thing today!"

"How do you usually determine who is allowed in? Does everyone have to ring up?"

"Oh, yes. And the young man who you are looking for? He told me he had a delivery for the Penthouse suite and when I called up, I was told to send him up!"

I hadn't heard this, that someone had OK'd sending him up.

"What was he delivering?" asked Knobs.

"I never ask! No, sir, this is not my business. People pay a lot of money to live here, not to have an old man getting his filthy fingers all over their deliveries! If the tenant, she says 'Send him up!' I send him up!"

"And what if he's delivering drugs?"

"People pay a lot of money to live here, not to have an old man calling the police because they enjoy relaxing after a hard day's work! And I tell you, I am very fond of Ms. Bathory and Ms. O'Farrel. But I see the bandages! With that going on under this roof, who am I to say anything about the drugs? Live and let live. That is what they pay me for!"

"But somebody's not living anymore, thanks to you," said Knobs. That jab from nowhere even caught me off guard.

Steve got right up into Knobs' face, or as close as his five foot frame would take him. "Not thanks to me! I did my job! I called up. She said send him up! Not thanks to me!"

Knobs was being a dick, but I saw what he was after so I didn't interfere. "But you're supposed to be security. You telling me this guy didn't ring any bells with you? You let a guy who was going to carve up one of your tenants walk right past you, and all you can say is 'I did my job?'"

"I did do my job!" Steve trembled with rage. "I warned her!"

"You warned her?" Now that was unexpected. I pushed. "How did you warn her?"

Pause. Brief glower. Recover.

"I am not in the habit of talking about this."

"You've already started. How did you warn her?"

Nothing.

"Steve," I said, "I'm not here as a cop. Ms. Bathory and Ms. Farrel — they're my friends. I don't know if I can do any good here, but please, help me try."

Suddenly the 'Steve!' persona went away, taking all the unnecessary exclamation points with it, and we found ourselves talking to Chukwuemeka. The smiling doorman working for Christmas tips made way for the serious security professional hidden behind his sunny mask. Between the excellent acting skills and the military posture, I found myself wondering how Chukwuemeka Obgweh had made his living in Nigeria. "Let's step outside," he said. "I would rather not be overheard talking about this. Tenants. Not very understanding sometimes."

I agreed and followed him outside, where he lit a cigarette. "I have been in this business—and other related businesses—for many years. I am retired from the related businesses, but I have my skills. Most of my tenants see me as a doorman. I let people in, I let people out. But some of the people who live in buildings like this—the rich, the famous, the infamous —are concerned about precisely who comes in and who gets out. Now, this is not corporate security. These are not international men of mystery. These are real people with inflated profiles. And this is where they live. We cannot install biometric scanners and metal detectors. Providing lifestyle security requires a more subtle set of skills than that. The kind of skills one acquires working in palaces. Compounds. Embassies. You understand?" Of course we did. "My tenants also desire the illusion that they come and go with complete freedom and normality. Providing the velvet prison cell they demand becomes something of a game. So I and my similarly experienced colleagues play that game. For instance, we use many casual code phrases to… well… to reduce the drama. Different codes with different clients. Or I should say 'tenants.' Different public profile, different priorities, you follow?" I nodded. Ertzbeth was an extraordinarily private worldwide celebrity vampire. I could see that her security requirements would be somewhat unique. "Should someone call on Ms. Bathory—or any of a number of other… priority… tenants—and that someone does not pass my personal sniff test, I announce the visitor as 'a nice-looking young man' or 'a pleasant young woman.' My tenants have learned to trust my judgment on these things." I bet they had.

"Yesterday a delivery man arrived. In my judgment he was deliberately avoiding our security cameras, as well as my scrutiny. I called upstairs and said 'A nice-looking gentleman has a delivery for you.' All she said was 'Yes? Send him up.' Now, I tell you again, I did not trust this man at all. I said 'Yes, he is very good-looking. What should I do?' And she cut me off. "Yes? Send him up.' What choice did I have?"

"I'm sorry I got in your face," said Knobs. "I like that system." Obgweh's cold stare made it clear he neither sought nor cared one way or the other about Knobs' approval.

"Are you sure you spoke with Ms. O'Farrel?" I asked.

"No. Ms. O'Farrel had gone running a few minutes earlier. I spoke with Ms. Bathory."

In the middle of the afternoon. An Elder vampire answering the phone. Not unheard of, but about as likely as hitching a ride with an Orthodox Rabbi on a Saturday. According to Ertzbeth herself, she was taking her usual midday nap when she was attacked.

"Do you prefer Chukwuemeka?"

"Steve really is fine. Too many mispronunciations of Chukwuemeka are obscene in Yoruba. Steve is safer."

"You speak English very well."

"It is the national language of Nigeria. Perhaps someday you Americans will learn it."

OK. Time to get us back on track. "Steve, do me a favor. Let's go back inside and call up to Ms. Bathory's apartment."

"But no one is there."

"I know that. Humor me. Let's just do it."

Steve tamped out his cigarette, tossed it into a nearby waste barrel and led the way inside. There, he picked up his security phone, punched in Ertzbeth's intercom number and waited. He gestured that it was just ringing and ringing when suddenly his eyes flew wide and he pulled the phone away from his face as if it had bitten him.

"Is it Ms. Bathory?" I asked.

"But how can she...?" Realization dawned and he cut loose with a string of Yoruba obscenities. I assume. It could have been a really pissed off shopping list for all I knew. I took the phone from him. Sure enough, it was Ertzbeth's voice. Recorded, no doubt. On a loop. She said 'Yes?' And then five seconds later, 'Send him up.' I waited. The sequence repeated. Clearly that's what Steve heard when he gave his second warning. "Yes? Send him up."

I called Lord B and asked him if a BNA comms team had dug into the building's systems. Of course not. They'd been so focused on blood and ballistics they'd only spoken to Steve long enough to get the penthouse master key. I told B to get an electronic forensics team into the security system as soon as possible. It had been compromised and I wanted our guys to give it the once-over before the building's network provider got its hands all over it.

If I'd been wondering what the hell I was doing there in the middle of the night, pissing with the federal big dogs (and I sort of was) I stopped worrying the moment I heard Ertzbeth's voice. I figure if I can patch a hole in their investigation before I even get past the front desk, the BNA big dogs are just gonna have to make a little room.

We headed for the private elevator to the penthouse. It was the only elevator our killer could have used. Behind us, Obgweh was still reeling out his shopping list of obscenities. As the elevator door shut, I heard him smash the receiver against the front desk and berate himself for being conned. "She would have been asleep! ASLEEP!"

"If Shelly and I ever make enough to afford a doorman," said Knobs, "I want that guy."

We scoped out the elevator box. Spacious, real wood, rounded security mirrors mounted on the back wall. I pulled my jacket over my head to block the ambient light and peered into glass panels integrated into the wood panel design. Yep. Two-way mirrors. Through them I could barely make out small black security cam lenses mounted high behind the wall, just below the ceiling of the car. From that angle, the cameras covered virtually every inch of the passenger space. Unfortunately, anyone with a need for anonymity could hide his face simply by standing right beneath one in a brimmed hat. B's team would certainly scour the security files, but any amateur could slip by these cams. The same problem had been evident in the foyer outside the elevator. A little black camera dome winked directly overhead. Walk with a ball cap pulled low, pretending to read a newspaper or just fiddling with your keys, and the cameras would get nothing but a great shot of the bill of your cap. As long as you were smart enough to eschew logos and name tags, you could walk under these babies all day and never offer a clue to your identity. I could see why Obgweh was so touchy about his personal security responsibilities. He was a 21st century pro stuck working with 20th century technology.

Getting to the penthouse floor had proven depressingly easy. The tough part for any unwanted visitor, though, would be getting into Ertzbeth's apartment. The floor between the elevators and her door was marble. The ceiling was a marble parabolic arch. Every step echoed. Even Knobs' sneakers made a loud "Pock! Pock! Pock!" as we crossed the foyer. Ertzbeth would hear anything short of a ninja the second he stepped off the elevator. Then there was the door itself. She had recently had a custom security door installed. It appeared to have been inspired by the castle doors that had kept angry Eastern European mobs at bay during her childhood. Three-inch thick oak, reinforced with steel inside and out. A digital keypad controlled a ten-inch deadbolt. Nothing short of a battering ram would get through. Fortunately, B was as good as his word, and one of his people had unlocked the door for us prior to our arrival. Just inside the door, a sixty-pound mahogany bar leaned against the wall. Wrought iron brackets flanked the door jamb. When both women were home, they could literally bar the gates from the inside against intruders. Old habits.

Despite my lucky break downstairs, there was no use kidding ourselves that we were going to find some physical evidence the BNA techs had overlooked. But just for shits and grins we searched the place one more time.

Virtually the entire living space of 'Beth's 2,500 square foot apartment had been given over to Peggy's exercise equipment. Where others might put a baby grand piano, Peggy had set up a fully-equipped Universal weight training rack. Just outside the kitchen, she had a Muay Thai banana bag and speed bag rack. Beneath the bay windows overlooking the Hudson River, she had a rower—one of the old-fashioned ones with the wooden skids. Instead of the exotic carpets and artwork you'd expect in a $1.5 million penthouse suite, Peggy had exercise mats, a floor-to-ceiling mirror and a ballet barre. A jump rope was casually wrapped around the terrace railing. No treadmill. Peggy ran outdoors in any kind of weather.

A leather loveseat, stereo and 50-inch HDTV were crammed together on a 12-by-12 square Persian carpet at the wall farthest from the master bedroom.

The profusion of fitness gear spoke volumes about the relationship between Ertzbeth and Peggy, and reminded me of a conversation we'd had just a few months earlier. Following the Cheeky Chekowicz debacle of last year, Ertzbeth had started making frequent visits to Hawthorne—once with Lord B, twice with Peggy—but usually solo. We'd make dinner at home and just chat about... well, stuff. TV. Sports. Project Runway. CSI Miami. Nascar. Casual people stuff. Elder vampires don't often get to make small talk. At first, it was a little daunting. 'Beth is a sensory overload, and virtually royalty among her own kind. But she seemed to cherish the experience of being just 'Beth instead of The Blood Countess. And very quickly, we found ourselves cherishing her company, too.

After dinner one night, just the three of us—Jonathan Coulton would call us my beloved and my millionaire girlfriend and I—we sprawled in front of the fire in our family room, enjoying a glass of wine. 'Beth was in a particularly introspective mood.

"We are what we are," she said. "Parasites. All living things are parasites. It is nothing to be ashamed of. But we unliving things, oh, we excel at it. I do not take blood any more. You know this. No more the Blood Countess. Just your 'Beth. When I drink fresh blood, from the tap, as it were, it is a gift. From my sweet Peggy. You know this, as well. I never take too much. Just a sip to make our love making sweeter." With that, my beloved bride Tami, knowing me as well as she does, immediately placed a pillow over my lap.

"Oh, does this talk of women in love make you uncomfortable, my dear Angus?"

"No, I am just fine." I pulled the pillow from my lap, thought twice and put it back. Tami and Ertzbeth erupted in ripples of giggles.

She continued. "So it is not the blood depletion that fatigues you mortals. We Wampyr, we set a different pace. We move faster, more forcefully, and of course we are much stronger than you. And that can make it dangerous to be around us, even when we mean no harm."

"Peggy seems happy," Tami ventured.

"As am I. I have not loved like this for many years. Generations. I loved Peggy as a child—as an adult should love a child—and now that she is a woman, I love her as a woman can love a woman. She is desperately precious to me, like sunshine is to you. And I know she feels the same. But still, I exhaust her. She exercises every day to be strong for me. To be fast and hard and tough. And yet, I must hold her like a china doll. When we make love, she clutches at me with all her strength, and she believes I do the same. And I want to. When we are skin to skin I want nothing more than to forget the world and crush her in my arms—but if I forget for a second that she is not Wampyr, that is exactly what I would do. Crush her in my arms."

And so Peggy worked to be as hard and resilient as she could be, just so she could be soft in the arms of her love.

Now Peggy was gone. And Ertzbeth was alone, again.

My chest had gone tight, my breathing wet. Knobs stared at me, tapping his watch. I shook off the memory and focused on the job at hand.

• • • • •

Careful not to disturb anything, we scanned the living room. While fitness seemed to be the dominant decorating theme, other personal touches told an intimate story of the two women who had shared a life here. Cameras of all types and ages were on display all over the apartment. I picked up a Premo folding bellows camera. My granddad had had one when I was a kid, and it had been an antique then. This one was in perfect condition, and it appeared to be one of the newer cameras in the room. Every shelf, every flat surface, hosted a camera or lens assembly. By comparison, there were relatively few photos—perhaps three or four per camera. But oh, the variety: black and whites, tintypes, daguerreotypes, Polaroids. All exquisitely matted and framed. I'd be willing to bet every photo in the place had been taken by Ertzbeth on these very cameras, when they were brand new.

One place of honor on the wall nearest the bedroom held a half-dozen black and white shots of Peggy. Five were stunning art shots of her working out. Stretching at the barre. Sweating on the vertical press, moonlight glistening on her long muscles. In almost all, she was gorgeously naked or topless. But in one, she wore a long silk gown with pearls. She stood on the terrace on a moonlit night, grinning ear-to-ear. Her fair Irish skin glowed in the moonlight. It must have been a long exposure, because I couldn't see any flash bounce off the marble terrace wall. And whereas all the other photos in the apartment were perfectly cropped, this photo was off-center. Peggy stood left of center, her left hand grasping something... And then I saw it. A translucent aura stood next to her, kissing her cheek. I looked closer and could barely make out Ertzbeth herself, wrapped around Peggy like a light human fog. They must have stood there together, stock still, for hours in the pitch dark, in front of a wide-open shutter, to register this ethereal hint of the elder vampire on film.

I put the Premo back where I'd found it and went to find Knobs. I caught up with him at the bedroom door. Crouching, he pointed to a faint red spot on the hardwood floor. A very faint trail of blood—seven tiny splatters in all—described a line from the master bedroom across the floor and out the front door. The trail led right over Peggy's weight bench, which suggested her killer was going fast enough, and feeling spry enough, to jump the bench rather than work his way around it. Even through a Kevlar vest, a shotgun blast is devastating. If he was running, he was one tough son of a bitch.

We checked the bedroom. Here the blood spatter was, of course, much worse. Any observer who hadn't yet heard Ertzbeth's story would reasonably assume that all the day's violence had taken place at the doorway and the side of the bed. The techs had carefully bagged every bit of flesh and bone the killer had cut from 'Beth as evidence, leaving no trace of the atrocity that had been committed on the unstained white satin sheets.

I studied the bedroom, looking for anything out of place. I'd only been there once before. That time, it was I who was battered and beaten, and 'Beth who was tending to my injuries. She'd been helping us chase a lead when I took a couple of pretty bad falls. Down a mountain, actually. Dislocated my hip, broke my nose. You know. Typical overnight shift. Turns out Ertzbeth is a big believer in therapeutic massage. She's good at it, too. I'd still be limping today if not for her. She just caught me a little by surprise with her old-fashioned morality. When I say old-fashioned, I mean really old-fashioned. She insisted that warriors going into battle together were obliged to bathe together first. To make a long story short, even if I hadn't been battered into a fog at the time, I doubt I'd have remembered much about 'Beth's apartment. When she wants a man's undivided attention, the walls could catch fire and he might not notice.

"Knobs, how's your memory of this place? Does anything look out of place?"

"You kidding me? I was offered the second-best shower, a towel and a hot cup of joe. You were the stud with the personal tour of the bedrooms. Did you ever tell Tami about that shower?"

"I sure did, before Ertzbeth could beat me to it. They both thought I was 'cute' about it. We'll see how cute it is when Ertzbeth finally gets Tami into a shower stall..."

Knobs just stared at me. "You know..."
"Don't."
"You brought it up."
"Not what I meant..."
"But 'Beth is..."
"We should get back to work."
"Good idea."

"Jesus. Timing, Knobs."

A column of semi-circular cherry wood shelves stood next to the right side of the bed. Each shelf held a camera and a photo. Based on the content of the photos and the apparent ages of the cameras it didn't seem too much of a stretch to assume the photos had been paired with the cameras that had taken them. One shelf, at just about shoulder height, held only a photo. It looked like a daguerrotype. The subject was a plump and pretty young girl, sitting primly in a high-backed Shaker chair. Knees and ankles together, hands folded in her lap, a sweet innocent smile on her trusting face. The only element out of place was her white left breast, exposed by her unbuttoned blouse. On the breast were two dark wounds. Yep. Definitely a Bathory original.

But where was the camera? The photo stood in a dark wooden frame at the left edge of the shelf, as if it usually shared space with something. I pointed it out to Knobs.

"I don't think somebody broke into Fortress Bathory to steal an old camera."

"Then where's the camera? You think Erztbeth loaned it out to the local shutter club?"

"What does it matter? Nobody stalks vampires to steal cameras. It's like stalking a horse to steal his tricycle."

"What?"

Knobs shook his head. "Whatever. You know what I mean. Why would you even assume he had one?"

"I get you. But how many facts did we have coming in here?" I asked.

"About, oh... zero."

"And now we have slightly more than zero. I think that's time well spent. The guy stole a camera. Maybe he's a killer and a kleptomaniac."

"Maybe he's in the AV club at P.S. 109."

I hate sarcasm unless it's mine. "You find anything else of use?"

"No."

"Then shut the hell up."

Knobs was probably right. So the guy stole a camera? So what? But the trip to World Wide Plaza wasn't a waste. We got a chance to say goodbye to Peggy.

6

As we passed Giants Stadium, my cellphone rang.

"Angus, how is she?"

"Pretty bad, Angel. But she'll heal. She's good at it. You know about Peggy?"

Tami got quiet for a few seconds. Probably offering a prayer to the Goddess. "B called. Angus, how are they going to get you on this case?"

"You want me on it?"

"Don't screw with me. I know it's not your jurisdiction. Pull whatever strings you have to pull. She's family."

"Family. I hear you, Baby."

I walked up my own driveway as the sun was rising. My sweetheart, buff and beautiful in jeans and a scrub shirt, met me at the door with a hot cup of decaf. "I'm on my way out. I left you bacon and there's whole wheat. Make yourself some eggs and go to bed! B left a message. He'll meet you at the station at dusk." She pulled out her smart phone. "Sun sets at 7:35 tonight."

I put my finger over her mouth, wrapped my other arm around her and squeezed. She tossed the phone on the counter and squeezed back. All the knots in my back popped. God, that felt good. Tami's a physical therapist working out of Valley Hospital in Ridgewood.

When we met, nearly twenty years ago, I had no idea how handy her skills would eventually become around the house. I dropped both hands onto her butt, hoisted her up so she was sitting on my hips, and started kissing her neck like I hadn't seen her in a week. "I have to go!" she shrieked, pushing herself away.

"Fine," I said, grabbing the back of her belt and hoisting her over my shoulder. "Go to work. Your husband needs some R&R but you're off to care for the sick and wounded. You're a cruel woman with twisted priorities." I carried her to her car.

"You, sir...stop that! Hey. HEY! Stop and look at me."

I put her down.

"I know how you get. You are exhausted. And very upset. And you think if you act like the jungle stud I know you can be I won't worry about you."

"Angus want Tami! Now! Work later."

Slapping my roving hands, "Let go of that. I need that. Angus, it's OK. I know how you feel right now. And I know in my heart that you and Knobs are going to catch this guy. I don't care how many FBI or BNA agents they get on it. They're going to need you and Knobs. Ertzbeth and Peggy are family. No one messes with the Wellstones."

"Not more than once, at least."

"You'd think they'd learn huh? Take your hand off that. The neighbors are looking."

"Sorry."

"No. You're not. Get some food. Get some sleep. Then get to work."

Sounded like a plan.

• • • • •

I woke up around 3 p.m. and checked my voicemails.

One from B. One from my boss, Commander Todd. They weren't happy with each other. Fuck 'em. Let them fight over jurisdiction. I needed to sweat. I called Knobs. "Hey, Knobs? You up for a workout?"

"Like you wouldn't believe. We'll meet you at the Dog Run."

I suited up, grabbed my keys and drove over to Goffle Park. It's a three-mile long stretch of green running along the Goffle Brook. It's a pretty trail to run, but it's pretty secluded, too. Too many trees on both sides blocking the view from the road. Last year Tami got attacked there, so Knobs and I make sure to run it occasionally. Establishing a police presence keeps everybody just a little more honest.

The running path begins at a large dog run. When I pulled in, Knobs was nuzzling with a gigantic blond wolf with piercing blue eyes while stretching out his calf muscles. He had a small knapsack on his back. I walked by, gave Knobs a clap on the shoulder and kissed Shelly on the muzzle. "Hi, baby. How you feelin'?" She licked my face and wagged her tail. "You guys up for a run?" They both fell in beside me and we took off down the lane.

"Shelly, I'm going to have to borrow Knobs from you for a few days." The dog yipped. "He told you what happened to Ertzbeth. B's managing to "borrow" us for the duration of the case. Commander Todd's not happy, and she wants in on all briefings. We're caught in a little bit of a turf war, but at least we're in."

She yipped again. "Oh, yeah, you better believe it. I'm too old to hotdog a case like this. And I'll try to keep Knobs on a short leash—no offense."

The dog barked twice at Knobs and scampered through an opening at the bottom of a hedge. Knobs stopped, took off the knapsack and shoved it in after her. In just a few minutes, a blond woman in a T-shirt pushed through the hedge, tying the lace on her running shorts. "You think this is funny, Angus," Shelly said, handing the knapsack back to Knobs. "Thanks, Honey. Listen, I love 'Beth as much as you two do, but the last time you got mixed up with Lord B, Knobs and Tami almost died and I got this." She pointed to a large square patch of slightly discolored skin on her throat. It used to be the site of a gaping hole, until a quick-thinking Israeli doctor applied a Golem Patch and saved her life. She survived the attack, and is still adjusting to life as a werewolf.

"This is different," said Knobs. "That was a demon!"

"And this is a guy who can go toe to toe with The Blood Countess.

Don't tell her I called her that."

"I won't. Baby, we don't really have a choice," said Knobs. "There just aren't that many experts on this stuff. It's too new. Angus knows this shit better than any other non-Nocturnal."

"That's not true," I protested. Although I suspected it was true.

"Yes it is. Honey, it's not like Angus is some kind of genius or anything..."

"Thanks..."

"No problem. But he's got an understanding, in his gut, of how to fight these new kinds of battles. And if he goes, I have to go, because at the old kind of battle, he's a total pussy. I gotta watch his back."

Shelly became very still. She stared at me for nearly a minute, her face stony and unreadable. She absently slipped her fingers under the waistband of her shorts and held her hands flat on her muscular belly for a few seconds as she just stared into our eyes. First mine, her ice-blue eyes pinning me like a butterfly in wax. Then Knobs'. Her pupils shifted ever so slightly canine, growing deeper, richer, and harder, like a protective bitch. (I say that with all due respect.) Then she suddenly softened, gave Knobs a hug, kicked off her shoes, pulled off her t-shirt and shorts and stood there, naked, her face just six inches from mine. "He gets hurt," she pointed at Knobs, "you're Dog Chow. Race ya!" And she exploded into full wolf form, snapped the air a hair's breadth from my nose, turned and ran down the trail. I ran after her, leaving Knobs to pick up her gear.

7

"Hey, Angus, Tami's on 223. You in the middle of anything?" Sergeant Clawfoot Pierowski stuck his gigantic head into the Station briefing room. I looked around the conference table. At the head was our police chief, Commander Leah Todd. Standing next to her was Lord B, the co-Director of the Bureau of Paranormal Affairs, just in from Washington, D.C.. Knobs was sitting next to me. On the table spilled a pile of reports, two laptop computers, six evidence bags and four cups of coffee. Tacked to the wall were two dozen photos of all the wounds inflicted upon Ertzbeth Bathory by the phantom guest of honor at our little briefing party.

I just pointed at everything. "OK," he said. "How 'bout I tell her you'll call her back?"

"Is it important?"

"No, she said she could talk to you later."

"That's what I'll do then. Thanks, Sarge."

Sergeant Clawfoot Pierowski is 50% Polish, 50% Seneca and, when the moon is full or the Jets are losing, 100% raging lycanthrope. And he hates it when we have closed door meetings in the briefing room.

"Can I get you guys anything?"

"No, we're good Sarge," said Knobs.

"Pleasure to see you again, Mr. Ruthven."

Lord B smiled and nodded.

"Chief, my shift is over in about a half hour. If you need some backup on... whatever it is you're working on..." He craned his neck to read over Knobs' shoulder. Knobs smiled and closed his folder. "Well, I just want to remind you that I am available and more than willing..."

I got up. "Sarge. Clawfoot. Relax. I promise as soon as we have somebody we need stepped on, you're our go-to guy."

"I just worry about being... you know... overlooked."

Knobs got up. "Jesus Christ! 'Foot, you're about seven and a half feet tall and you turn into a grizzly bear when you're pissed off! A grizzly bear with a riot stick!"

"Kodiak Bear."

"What's the difference?"

"Kodiaks are bigger."

"There you go! You are officially impossible to overlook without an extension ladder. Now get the hell out of here!" Knobs put his shoulder against Pierowski's belly and started to shove. Pierowski didn't budge. Knobs pinched a tendon just above Pierowski's kneecap that made him step back and howl.

"Ohhhh GEEZ I hate that! You son of a bitch!" But by then the door was closed.

Lord B asked, "Do you have to take that call?"

"No, she said to call her back. Keep going, B."

"Good. Let's get back to the DNA screening. The blood was very difficult to isolate since so much of it belonged to poor Ms. O'Farrel. We know so far for a certainty that the attacker was a white male."

"'Beth told you that."

"Yes, Knobs, and now we have confirmed it, as well."

"He is of western European descent."

"Which would make him... a white male. Angus, you're under arrest."

'You'll never take me alive."

"OK."

"Are we done?" asked Commander Todd.

"Yep."

"The attacker showed impressive skill, not only in stalking an Elder vampire, but in compromising sophisticated communications systems at the Plaza and hacking the electronic lock on Ertzbeth's door. These skills are rare and very expensive to learn. Both the digital sound equipment he used to override the building's communications system and the UV scope he used to read Peggy's fingerprints on the digital deadbolt appear to be military issue. Worth thousands on the black market. Not at all unattainable, but expensive. Now Angus, you've got some information you wanted to discuss."

"When we checked out the apartment, I discovered that one camera had been removed. Now, I don't know antique cameras from a hole in the ground so I talked to some people. It turns out there's no real money in antique cameras. Folks collect them, but for their historical value, never as investments. With a few exceptions, they're just too common. So why steal a camera of little or no value while you're in the middle of taking down the most dangerous prey on the planet? Well it turns out there are a small number of extremely valuable antique cameras. And Ertzbeth owned one of them. She obtained a reverse mirror camera—a sophisticated camera obscura—from Louis Jacques Mandes Daguerre in 1840. This daguerrotype..." I held up the photo of the young girl with the pierced breast. "...was taken with that camera. It's one of the first cameras built for Daguerre, the father of photography. It's priceless."

"So he's a camera buff?" Asked Commander Todd. "He killed a girl because he wants an old camera?"

"No. Not at all. I think—and yeah, this is my gut talking, but go with it—the camera was a consolation prize. He wanted information about where Ertzbeth and her friends have squirreled away their wealth. Those were the final questions he kept asking, over and over. And remember, he must have spent quite a bit of cash planning and executing his invasion of Ertzbeth's home. That's an investment like any other, right? When his plan to get the information was literally blown away, he grabbed something—anything—of value to keep the trip from being a complete financial washout."

"So where does this lead us?" asked Todd.

B took over again. "There's one man who we know has the skills, the resources and the experience to stalk an Elder vampire. We also know that he's hungry for new revenue sources."

"I told you, you're under arrest, Angus."

"You're close, Knobs." Said Lord B.

"I'm what?"

"You're close. But whereas the police business has been booming since we signed the Twilight Statutes, our suspect's business has been effectively banned."

Knobs sat up straighter than a four year old waiting for pie. "You're killing me here, B. Who's our guy?"

"Van Helsing. Maarten Van Helsing."

8

"Wait a minute." Knobs interrupted. "I thought Van Helsing was one of the good guys."

B's nostrils flared. "He destroyed vampires for a living. I guess 'good guy' depends on your perspective. I might, for instance, call him a total bloody bastard."

"No! No, I'm talking about back in the day. When he went up against Dracula. I mean... Dracula. You can't defend Dracula."

"One," Lord B began, using a grade school teacher voice calculated to drive Knobs bananas, "There was never a vampire named Dracula. He was an amalgam of many vampires, whose executions at the hands of Van Helsing were blended and fictionalized into a book by Bram Stoker. Van Helsing saw the novel, correctly, as an excellent form of advertising for his services."

"So Dracula was an infomercial," I volunteered.

"Two, this is not that Van Helsing. Abraham Van Helsing died a very wealthy, very old man in his home in the Netherlands. Over one hundred years ago. And three, he was not the first Van Helsing to hunt vampires. Nor the last. In front of you is a profile of the current heir to the Van Helsing reputation."

I flipped through my briefing file until I reached a clipped stack of sheets headlined:

PROFILE: Maarten Van Helsing:
Born: 1960 (?)
Raised: The Netherlands
Father: Rutger Van Helsing (Deceased)
Mother: Hanna Otterbridge (Deceased)
Height: 6' 6"
Weight: 165 lbs
Hair: Gray (orig. Brown)
Distinguishing Characteristics:

Scars (large): left eye, chin, right cheek, left ear lobe, trachea, bridge of nose, chest (left nipple missing), right knee, left knee, right forearm.

Scars (small): Upper lip, left cheek (multiple) hands (many)

Scars (ritual) Pentagram - right breast; evil eye - right palm; ankh - inside mouth;

Missing: Left fifth toe; right pinky.

• • • • •

"Holy SHIT this guy's one ugly S.O.B."

"Keep reading, amigo," I said. "It gets better. This guy's a piece of work." Knobs started flipping through the dozens of pages in his briefing.

"Can you just summarize? I promise I'll do the homework when we get out of here. Who is this guy?"

"Maarten Van Helsing is the great-great-something-or-other-grandson—seven generations removed—of Abraham Van Helsing. For more than four hundred years, the Van Helsings have accumulated a sizable fortune as vampire hunters."

"I guess people would pay a fortune to be rid of them, right?" Commander Todd was scowling like she smelled something filthy on the bottom of her shoe. "No offense intended, Mr. Ruthven." I didn't know if she was disgusted with Van Helsing or with the idea of stopping him. In general, Todd keeps her cards close to the vest. And as a rule, she doesn't call anyone "Lord" or "Lady" anything.

She stands just over five feet tall and weighs about 180. Nearly sixty years old, she benches 250. She keeps her steel-gray hair cut short in what I guess you'd call a "Prince Valiant" if it weren't so curly. She's one of the few African-American police chiefs in New Jersey, and the only woman.

"Offense taken anyway, Commander. You will have to pardon me, but this family has made a practice of hunting down my kind, regardless of our own behavior. Yes, Dracula—or whichever vampire inspired the character—was a vicious criminal. But many of my kind had turned their backs on human prey long before the Purges. A rare few had never taken up the practice at all! And still the Van Helsings hunted. They were accidental heroes at best. Cold-blooded killers at worst."

"I'm sorry you feel that way, Mr. Ruthven," Todd stood her ground. "We'll have to agree to disagree. Before modern times, we mortals were entirely outclassed by your kind. Without laws in place, without police protection, without the Twilight Statutes and people like my own officers here... Well, I can understand how the Van Helsings thought they were doing the right thing."

"Then why did they loot the castles and vaults they hunted in?"

"Excuse me?"

"The peasants and gypsies of Eastern Europe could not afford to pay the Van Helsings. Few could afford them today! At best they could offer a few chickens, or a night with their daughter. These heroes would use the hunt as an excuse to loot the graves and mausoleums of the very villages they were hired to protect."

"But hadn't the vampire stolen the treasure first?" I asked. "The Van Helsings were just stealing from thieves."

"And that makes it better? Robin Hood would have given the money back to the people. The Van Helsings rode off, leaving the villages poorer than when they had arrived. But it gets worse. Often they would torture the vampire first to learn where he had hidden his family fortune."

"You think that's what happened with Ertzbeth?" she asked.

Ruthven slapped the table, leaving a crack in the top. "I KNOW that is what happened! I was at Vesuvius when we put an end to Francis Varney!" B paused, saw the damage he'd done to the table and collected himself. "Varney was an animal who had plundered his victims' homes and blackmailed wealthy families by threatening their children. We put him down after more than 100 years of unchecked murder. But unlike the Van Helsings, we chose not to profit from the act. So we returned what we could, and buried the rest."

"What has Varney got to do with Van Helsing?" I asked.

"Abraham Van Helsing was there! It was Ertzbeth and myself who threw the bag of corruption into the volcano. Varney. Not Van Helsing. We foolishly cooperated with the Van Helsings, thinking they would rejoice at our rehabilitated state. It was the first and only time I've lain eyes on a Van Helsing."

B told Knobs to lock the door, then reminded us all that this was a top-secret briefing.

[I've since gotten permission from all the parties involved to tell the story here, in as close to Lord B's own words as I can recall—A. Wellstone.]

[Detective Wellstone has a keen ear for facts, but a tin ear for the finer gracenotes of dialogue. I have taken the liberty of correcting his recollections.—Lord Victor Ruthven]

9

Lord B's Story

I left England in 1816, at the age of 28, running from debts, unwanted children and other scandals too numerous to list. My name—as I am sure you have all long known—was George Gordon Noel Byron. Lord Byron. Poet, seducer, and callous bon vivant. My face and facility with language had earned me universal adoration, which I, of course, arbitraged for sexual excess. Though by any rational measure I was still a young man, my character was curdled like an old prisoner unjustly jailed. So cruel and vile was I to those who loved me that my own physician, John Polidori, infuriated and humiliated beyond endurance, penned a parody of me, which he called The Vampyre. By the age of 36, I was an exile on the Continent, using my money and reputation to attach myself like a lamprey upon whatever literary souls would tolerate my bad behaviour.

One night, having inveigled an invitation to stay with the Shellys in Geneva, Mary, infuriated by some acidic comment, threw a copy of The Vampyre at me. "Polidori was right" she said. "You, my Lord Ruthven, are a leech."

Although, on the advice of my advocates, I had sued Polidori over The Vampyre, I had never actually read it. Since not one of my friends was presently speaking with me, Mary had locked all the absinthe away, and I had no ready cash with which to hire a whore, I pulled a chair up before the fire and read a vision of myself, as reflected in my victim's eyes.

"He gazed upon the mirth around him," Polidori had written, "as if he could not participate therein. ... In spite of the deadly hue of his face, which never gained a wanner tint, either from the blush of modesty, or from the strong emotion of passion, though its form and outline were ... it was not upon the virtuous... that he bestowed his alms; -- these were sent from the door with hardly suppressed sneers; but when the profligate came to ask something, not to relieve his wants, but to allow him to wallow in his lust, to sink him still deeper in his iniquity, he was sent away with rich charity."

So this is how I was perceived. As a Vampyre. As a cold flame that consumed without giving warmth. Reading Polidori's book felt like looking in a mirror for the very first time. Although his story told of a mythical creature (or so we all thought) every word described the all-too-mortal libertine begging board and bath of old friends as I squirreled my own wealth away and allowed my children to struggle for sustenance back in England.

I decided that very night (after smashing open the absinthe cabinet) that I would make amends. I would redeem the noble name of Lord Byron and leave a legacy of courage and selflessness. Through long hours of self-struggle I convinced myself it was not too late. The only proper course, I determined, was to return immediately to England, to approach my publishers with plans for new writing projects, and to arrange for a large portion of the proceeds to be put aside for the education of young Ada and any other stray Byronets who might be toddling the byways of Britain. The proper path clearly illuminated as if by a lighthouse on the horizon, I immediately signed up to fight for Greek independence from the Turks.

At the time, my facility for procrastination was the stuff of legend.

I contacted the London Greek Committee and volunteered my services and dwindling fortune. They sent me to the Ionian island of Cephalonia, a breathtaking Mediterranean paradise. Between cannon fusillades, that is. There I bought the services of a small army and navy and sailed for Missolonghi, ready to drive the Turks back into the sea. Along with the fleet of ships and small battalion of soldiers, I acquired a lovely young boy named Loukas Chalandritsanos. I purchased him as a personal assistant while in Cephalonia. Something about his long well-turned limbs, his soft hands, his thick black eyelashes, feminine cheekbones and insolently bowed lips reminded me of all of the essential qualities I had always admired in myself. To fill the long quiet evenings I read to the boy from The Vampyre. The story, and the tale of my redemption through the bitter book, seemed to delight him. By the time we finished planning the assault on Lapidos, I was desperately in love with Loukas. I longed as deeply to be a hero for him as I did to redeem my name in London. But neither was meant to be. Just weeks before the assault, I began suffering from chills, fevers and, finally, epileptic seizures. I lost all hope of participating in the liberation of Greece. By day, the doctor bled me to reduce the poisons in my system. He had no way of knowing that the boy, Loukas, was also draining me by night. Yes, that way. At first. But then in an altogether more intimate fashion. The boy who played the part of my assistant, slave and lover was in reality my master. He was Vrykolakos. Wampyr. Vampire.

When I finally died, drained nearly dry by continual leeching, Loukas waited by my graveside throughout the night, pulling my struggling undead corpus from the earth. With a laugh like breaking glass he held my writhing, starving body above his head and presented his new toy to the night. 'Twas then he rechristened me Victor Ruthven.

The vampire's journey is often one from innocence to evil. Mine was quite the opposite. Having lived as a spiritual vampire, I was reborn into a new respect for mortal life. Loukas tried to teach me to feed, but I resisted. Years my senior, he had the strength to force blood upon me. And so he did. If he had not, I would have wasted and perished. But I fought every drop and searched for any opportunity to escape. For many months, he kept me walled up in an old abandoned prison on the Mediterranean coast. At night he would feed and bring me enough drops to survive through another day, spitting them into my mouth like a mother bird. Some nights I would break free and run, but it was all part of his cruel game. He always found me by dawn, and forced me to spend the day cowering for shade in some roofless ruin.

Then one night the Van Helsings came. Abraham was a very young man at the time, barely into his teens, small and light, but wiry, tough, competent with horse and rifle, and keenly intelligent. Seven riders came in all: Abraham, his elder brother Rhys, who led the expedition, and five Greek mercenaries from my own former regiment.

Loukas, the arrogant little fool, stood and fought. While the superstitious Greeks hemmed us in with crosses, the Van Helsing brothers peppered us with silver shot, which brought us both howling to our knees in agony. Rhys bound us and questioned us for hours. Appearing so many years older than my sire, I was assumed to be the elder vampire, and so Rhys tortured me with garlic and silver. He demanded the locations of others of my kind. I would have gladly told him everything I knew at the first touch of silver. Alas, I knew nothing of my own kind, having been kept captive my entire short afterlife. So they tortured me some more. Finally, in the light of the approaching dawn, one of my former men recognized me.

"Byron!" he cried. And he and his companions ran to my side, cut my bonds and embraced me like the prodigal son returned. Of all the misapprehensions of that dreadful adventure, perhaps the worst was the Greeks' belief that I was some kind of hero of the revolution. They refused to let the Van Helsings do me further harm. Seeing their hero reduced to this shameful state by the vrykolakos Loukas, they quickly beheaded the boy vampire and burned his lovely little body.

"George Gordon, Lord Byron?" Abraham asked, brandishing a silvered sword at my heart. Apparently my notoriety had reached even the grade schools of Amsterdam.

"You have me at a number of disadvantages, sir." I tugged the shredded remains of my frock coat into a semblance of order, smoothed my trousers and brushed back my filthy hair.

Both of the Dutch hunters laughed, sheathed their swords, bowed low in mock respect and introduced themselves. Since this all took place nearly seventy years before Stoker put pen to paper, their family name meant nothing to me. They explained that they were "fearless vampire hunters." I explained that I was but an accidental vampire, seduced and transmogrified by the monster they had so efficiently dispatched. I swore I had no intention of preying upon mortals (as, indeed, I did not.) I pleaded my obvious ill-health as evidence of my willingness to forego human blood. And so, they refrained from ending my pitiful existence. Of course, I believed their motive was Christian charity (something I'd heard old women nattering about in the parlor as a child). Were I not still reeling from my transformation and dramatic deliverance, I would, perhaps, have trusted my inherently cynical instincts and seen through to their baser motives. I, as Lord Byron, was a very rich man. I, as vampire, was completely at their mercy. No one to turn to. No strength to run. No choice but to agree to whatever mad scheme in which the "fearless vampire hunters" chose to enlist me. And so I became a plaything to another set of monsters.

Having emerged from this adventure empty-handed, the brothers sought to identify new prey as quickly as possible. Word reached us through established family channels of a vicious English beast amok in Naples sporting a sizable reward for his destruction. When we arrived in Naples, we rendezvoused with the sponsor of the bounty. She was as exquisite a lady as I had ever seen. No, nor have seen since. And I believe with every sinew of my withered heart that she will reclaim every glimmer of her radiance before long. Yes, our contact was Ertzbeth Bathory. Though she did not reveal her name at the time, such are the resources and the obsessive scholarship of clan Van Helsing that they soon discerned her true identity.

We met her in an alley in Naples, on a foggy April night in 1825, shortly after midnight. While Rhys interrogated the fair young lady, Abraham scoured his pile of books, frantically glancing at Ertzbeth, making notes and consulting tome after tome. Eventually, he packed his books away and moved to introduce himself. He reached out a hand. Ertzbeth took it. Concealed in his palm was a rosary. With a sharp gasp of pain, Ertzbeth drew back her hand.

"My Lady Bathory, I am at your service. Or shall I call you Blood Countess?"

"If you do," she warned, gripping Abraham by the ends of his scarf, "you shall not leave this alleyway alive."

Abraham blanched, but did not give ground.

In the few short seconds of the exchange, Rhys had drawn a pistol and held it aimed squarely at Erzeth's head. She let the scarf drop.

"If this was to be a trap," Rhys began, "you have fallen into it yourself."

"It is a trap, I assure you. But not for you. And certainly not for me. I wish to trap Sir Francis Varney—known to the tabloids in England as Varney the Vampire."

"Varney the Vampire?" I said with a dismissive laugh. "There's no such person! He's a badly written character in a penny dreadful!"

"And such things cannot possibly exist," She mocked. "In fact, you are but dreaming this entire episode... from the depths of your tomb! Yes, I smell the fresh dirt upon you, bloodling. You are like me—but still young and stupid. Did you think yourself unique? There are many others like us. This penny dreadful, this "Feast of Blood," is not a work of fiction, but a thinly disguised biography. Sir Francis Varney gorges himself on innocents throughout Europe, then profits again from his crimes by publishing them in weekly installments! The man is beyond redemption."

"Why do you hunt your own kind?" Abraham asked.

"My reasons are my own. You know who I am. Despite your incomparable network of spies and business agents, you've not heard one squeal of complaint over my depredations."

"How do you know what our network reports?"

"You have heard no complaints because there has been naught to complain of. Varney, however, has been on the Van Helsing list for many years. As he has been on mine. He is an embarrassment and a danger to both of our peoples. He preys on yours and exposes mine.

You have been waiting for a bounty to make it worth your efforts. And here I am, with the promise of one thousand English pounds. I will even assist you."

I learned later that Ertzbeth had, while listening to the peasants read to her in her tower prison, experienced her own epiphany, and had long been searching for ways to survive without stalking humans as prey. And while she was disgusted by Sir Francis Varney's gluttonous rampage on its own merits, she also believed that dedicating her own strength and fortune to ending his carnage would bring her a small step closer to making amends for her own crimes. Never having challenged another vampire (we are, by nature, solitary creatures) she sought to enlist the aid of experts. And thus began a conspiracy that Ertzbeth and I have kept secret for more than a century and a half.

Our benefactress had done most of our preparation for us. She'd discovered Varney's hiding place in the hills outside Naples without alerting him. Our sole remaining task was to take him unawares and skewer him. Abraham, always the scholar, showed us the potential folly of our plan. According to Feast of Blood, a chapter of which he had amongst his research, Varney was a resurrector. He could be stopped, dismembered, beheaded and burnt, but the smallest drop of blood or ray of the full moon's light would trigger a regeneration process that would eventually restore his full vitality. We needed to stop him permanently. If not for the sake of humankind, for our own sakes. According his own memoirs, Varney held grudges. We needed either to do the job right the first time or to abandon the plan altogether.

While waiting for the Van Helsings to answer her summons, Ertzbeth had reconnoitered Varney's hiding places throughout Naples and the surrounding countryside. We used this information to harry him from place to place. Here, we placed garlic in a grave. There, holy water in a tomb. Never confronting him, we simply eliminated his options, cut off his escape routes and herded him into our trap. And what a theatrical trap it was. In all of Italy, we could think of but one place isolated enough, deadly enough, brimming with the elemental power we needed to eliminate any chance that Varney's remains would come into contact with human blood or moonlight:

The fiery pits of Mt. Vesuvius.

For nearly a fortnight we chased and harried Varney, careful to avoid a deadly confrontation until we could deliver the coup de grace over the volcano's rim. Our caution cost us dearly. One night, as we neared our goal, Varney took the offensive. Just at the cusp of dusk, mere seconds after the sun had dipped below the horizon, Varney hurtled from a hidden cave and attacked us like a rabid wolf. Ertzbeth fought bravely, but was no match for him. I fell quickly, literally thrown bodily down the mountainside. Clearly, we were not the madman's prey. He lurched after the younger Van Helsing. Abraham defended himself well. He fought in what we thought of as 'the Oriental way' —wielding a pair of silver knives on rapidly spinning chains. To give the boy his due, he was quite magnificent. He did little significant damage, but his incessant slashing at the beast's face, cutting of his flesh and smashing of his teeth, served to keep the monster howling in rage, and mostly at bay. Eventually, Varney circled around Abraham and reached Rhys, who greeted him with a two-foot wooden spike through the heart. As Varney died, he tore at the hunter's throat, coating them both in sticky, fresh red blood. Held together by Rhys' death grip on the spike and Varney's grip on him, they lay pinned to each other's corpses like a giant human canapé.

Abraham ran to his brother, frantically prying him from his killer. So tight was Rhys' grip that as Abraham rolled his body off the vampire, he pulled the spike with him. Covered in Rhys Van Helsing's blood, Varney began immediately to heal. We had mere moments to act before the beast that had nearly vanquished all of us would be back to his full destructive vitality. Ertzbeth and I each grabbed a leg and sprinted for the volcano's rim. Abraham leapt from his brother's side and chased us, clutching at the writhing vampire we carried. He ordered us to stop, "No! I want him! He must pay!" But Varney's thrashing told us how quickly he was healing, so on we ran. Neither of us relished the thought of refighting the same battle we'd just barely won at such great cost.

The closer we came to the rim, the more frantically the body between us squirmed. Finally, we reached the stone ridge overhanging the bubbling pit. Abraham caught up and snatched at Varney's jacket, snarling in rage. I grabbed the boy by the collar and tossed him behind us. As Ertzbeth and I catapulted Varney over the outcropping and into the seething lava below, the villain let loose a banshee wail and reached, one last futile time, for our throats.

We turned and saw Abraham staring at his brother's lifeless corpse. "Will he turn?" he asked, quietly and calmly.

I had absolutely no idea.

"Probably not," Ertzbeth replied. "But there is a chance."

"Please throw him in the volcano, then."

As I began to object, Abraham walked back and began emptying Rhys' pockets. He casually counted his brother's money and placed it in his own wallet. He read and sorted a hand full of paper scraps, shoving more than half back into the dead man's pockets. When he was finished scavenging through his brother's belongings, he stood and nodded to the body as if we were carters and the corpus was luggage.

We did as he asked. Together, we solemnly carried our one-time conspirator and gently rolled him into the pit. We turned back from the sad chore to find ourselves surrounded by six men—well, five men and a deadly young boy—armed with crossbows.

"Where is Varney's fortune?"

"What fortune?" I asked.

"Safe from treacherous hands," said Ertzbeth.

"Deliver to me the vampire's horde and I shall order my men..."

"My men!" I protested. Arrogant little prick.

"Shut up, Byron. Dead men give no orders. Give me Varney's treasure and I shall order my men to let you go. Disobey and we will continue the torture with which we began our acquaintance."

Suddenly I became aware of a low whispering, like a bee's buzz across a field. My attention drawn to it, I focused my attention as much as I was able. I made out words. "Cross your arms over your heart, duck your head and run as hard as you can. Cross your arms over your heart, duck your head and run as hard as you can. Cross your arms over..." over and over. It was Ertzbeth's voice, set low and deep in her throat, so soft that none but prey animals—or others like ourselves—might hear it. I glanced once her way. She nodded, crossed her arms, ducked her head… and a shot rang out! She bolted toward our betrayers! I was but a fraction of a second behind her. Our captors flinched for but a moment at the sudden noise. One fell. We ran. Hard and fast, straight at our enemies. Four wooden quarrels thudded home in our forearms. They were tipped with silver and burned our arms like red hot pokers, but they never reached our hearts and we never slowed. Plummeting down the hillside, we bowled over two of our attackers. (I am ashamed to say Ertzbeth had the presence of mind—or the heat of anger—to slash one throat as we passed while I, thinking of nothing but continued existence, simply ran.) By the time Abraham and the two remaining mercenaries had reloaded, we were nearly out of range. As a last quarrel thudded at my feet, a shot rang out from in front of me. I heard a scream behind and shouts of outrage. Another shot rang out from the same direction. We rounded a copse of trees to find three saddled horses, their reins in the hands of a tall cadaverous-looking thug in top hat and overcoat.

"Your steed, milady," he said, in a rich, booming Irish brogue better suited to a dancehall stage than a fog-enshrouded hillside.

"Thank you, Mr. Black. And where is Inspector Vidocq?" she asked, as she roughly wrenched my quarrel-pricked arm away from my chest and shoved each bolt the rest of the way through as deftly as if she were sewing a button on my sleeve. She completely ignored my womanly screams, an act of kindness for which I am still grateful. Her own wounds she treated in the same way, but with significantly more silent dignity.

"He is guarding the boat at Torre Annunziata," replied the dark giant. It slowly dawned on me that the exquisite lady at my side had planned this adventure with much more care than I had, heretofore, given her credit.

We mounted and rode off down the mountain. The mysterious Mr. Black drew a rifle from a saddle holster and took position to hold the path. We rode like the Wild Hunt itself, all night, desperate to reach the boat before dawn. I rode as one bred to the saddle; Ertzbeth as one with the horse. At times my eye could scarce separate rider from ridden, so attuned was the lady to the rhythms of her steed.

As the first glow crested the horizon, the mountain to our north providing no shelter, we entered the sleeping city of Torre Annunziata. Creeping our horses through narrow streets, dodging from shadow to shadow, we finally reached the harbor, just as the sun crested the roofs of the city and lit the docks ahead of us with deadly sunshine. We both dismounted and huddled between the horses for shade.

Ertzbeth pointed toward a small sloop not a hundred yards away. "That ship is our salvation, my friend. What say you to a final desperate, mad, burning dash to our deaths?"

"It just so happens I have no other plans for this Morning. After you, my Lady."

We gathered as much of our clothing around our exposed flesh as we could and braced ourselves for the searing pain of the Mediterranean sun. We stooped like sprinters, nodded to each other and bolted from the shelter of the horses.

"Countess! Turn back!" And without a moment's hesitation, she spun, grabbed me and hurtled us both back into the quickly diminishing shade. At the far end of the dock rippled a billowing wave of ivory. Below it I could barely make out a pair of black-clad legs, pumping furiously. Soon I saw what it was—a sail! In moments the yards and yards of billowing fabric reached our shrinking shelter and flowed over us like seafoam. Ertzbeth wrapped us both as tighly as newborn babes. Our savior grasped a loose tail of sailcloth and tugged. We ran where he tugged us, blindly stumbling down the long dock. We stopped, and he pushed. We tumbled onto a pitching deck, from which our anonymous champion rolled us down a short flight of stairs. I heard a wooden 'thunk' above my head, which I assumed was the slamming of a hatch. I was correct.

"Maintenant vous êtes sûr."

We struggled out of our canvas cocoon. Ertzbeth knocked on the hatch and called out "Merci. Merci pour l'aide, mon ami courageux!" We felt the boat lurch as it drifted away from the dock. Ertzbeth kissed my cheek, dropped her head unceremoniously into my lap and collapsed into a deep sleep. I joined her.

We had barely escaped with our unlives. But we had learned an expensive lesson: The Van Helsing clan was not to be trusted. For while they posed as heroes their purpose was as low as any common highwayman. Profit.

That adventure was the beginning of a long friendship between Ertzbeth and myself. It also engendered a conspiracy that has remained a secret until today. The Van Helsings know that Ertzbeth and I relied on the assistance of loyal associates that day. Mr. Black and Inspector Vidocq have both left descendants behind, who, perhaps, are aware of the Varney fortune. Yes, Francis Varney had, in fact, plundered a tremendous fortune—worth millions today—from the estates of his victims. And our girl had, in fact, discovered his secret places. In the onths following Varney's plunge, Ertzbeth and I returned whatever we could of the treasure to its rightful owners. Anonymously, of course. What we could not return, we reburied. Better gold and gems return to the earth from whence they came than fall into the hands of the treacherous Van Helsings.

10

"OK. I get it," said Todd. "This Van Helsing character is descended from a long line of utter bastards. He's the Long John Silver of vampire hunters, searching for buried treasure. But why would he waste the effort to steal a camera, when his attention should have been focused on getting his hands on millions of dollars in jewels and gold?"

"Because Van Helsings are ghouls by nature," B replied. "Torture and theft are ingrained. Taught from birth. If one Van Helsing can rifle the pockets of his own dead brother, another can easily torture a victim with the right hand while burgling with the left."

"Well I, for one, am convinced," I said. "Can we get a warrant on this?"

"I wouldn't go in front of a judge with this," said Todd. "Honestly, Ruthven, you've put us in a spot here. I believe you're right on the money, but your beef is with the dead guy who took down Dracula. You want us to go arrest a man because his great great great great grandfather was an asshole. No judge could possibly allow this as grounds for a search warrant, much less an arrest warrant."

"Then we go and gather the evidence we need," said Knobs.

"I assume your people are keeping tabs on Maarten?" I ventured.

"Of course. He might as well have a lojack lodged in his derriere. He is traveling as The Incredible Van Helsing…"

Knobs snorted coffee out of his nose. "Wow. Solid alias! Must be a bitch to keep up with him."

"Oh, it gets better. He is traveling the Renaissance Festival circuit."

"Huh-ZAH!"

Suddenly a picture formed in my head of our scarred and twisted killer, bent over Ertzbeth's mutilated body, wearing tights and a jester's cap. "B. You have got. To be. Shitting. Me."

"I shit thee not, sirrah. Think about it for but a moment, and it will almost make sense. This man has been raised from birth to be," B ticked off a list on his fingers, "an expert in swordplay, classic literature, hand-to-hand combat, and theatrics. He's an extraordinary horseman, an acrobat and a master at throwing any form of edged weapon. All for the sake of making him the preeminent—and most profitable—vampire hunter on the planet. Now, if you had spent thirty-five years mastering that precisely calibrated mix of skills, and suddenly, without warning, the entire world outlawed the only job you had been trained to do, where would you go, Angus? What would you do?"

"I don't know. I just can't see Van Helsing as a carnie."

"Not quite a carnie. He is what they call in the Festival business a 'main stage trunk show.' Apparently he is a one-man three-ring circus and makes thousands of dollars in tips and merchandise every weekend. Granted, it's a far cry from the days when his family was looting castles, but I'd be willing to bet he makes more than we poor civil servants do. When was the last time you were at a Renaissance Festival, Angus?"

I had to think hard about that. "It's got to be ten years," I said.

"Uh, for me," said Knobs. "that would be... never."

"Well, then! Enough talk. Commander Todd, I understand that you are reticent to assign men to investigate Van Helsing on such flimsy evidence. But I am sure you agree that these two hard-working men deserve a weekend off, to take their lovely ladies to the Faire?" At that, he pulled four tickets from behind Todd's ear.

"And now you're David fucking Copperfield." Todd got up,

opened the conference room door. "Alright, Mr. Ruthven, I see no reason why they can't visit this Renaissance Festival of yours. Gentlemen, feel free to submit expenses. If you can get receipts from the ale wenches. And if you happen upon the Incredible Van Helsing Show, you should pull up a hay bale and enjoy."

Sergeant Pierowski was passing by the doorway. "Van Helsing? That's what Tami wanted to talk to you about, Angus."

"What? What did she say?"

"That this guy, Van Helsing, had stopped by your house. Give her a call. He might still be there."

I ran for the parking lot, Knobs at my heels. I hit the little voice activation button on my cell phone "Call home." Ring. I hit the automatic unlock, opened the driver's-side door. Ring. Knobs got in the passenger side. Ring. I started the ignition as Tami picked up. "Hi, Baby." Caller ID.

"Tami, is he in the house?"

"Who?"

"Are you alone? Can you talk?"

"What are you talking... Oh. Yes, I'm alone. No. Really, I'm alone. Tall dark and handsome was here for about five minutes."

"Handsome?"

"Well, yeah. He was cute. In a tall, dark way. Are those your tires I hear squealing?"

I slowed down. "You sure he's gone?"

"I assume he's involved in Ertzbeth's case somehow?"

"We think he's the guy who did it."

"Oh, shit."

11

"Thou shalt not pass!" So said the giant with the wooden stick. Knobs smiled and kept walking. "Hold, sirrah!" said the leather-clad monolith, stepping in front of us again. "I be Little John, proud member of Robin Hood's Merry Band! And I say ye shall not pass 'til thou dost give me the secret password! Ha ha ha!" The crowd was eating it up. Knobs, not so much. There aren't many who can see the top of Knobs' head. This Little John guy was huge. With his long blond hair and yellow beard, he looked more like Thor than an English peasant. No doubt Knobs could break him in half, but for what? Improvising without a license?

Knobs and I both casually pulled our overshirts aside to show our badges. Little John flung his mane dramatically and delivered his line over the shoulder, directly to his appreciative audience. "Oh, so thou dost work for the Sheriff of Nottingham! Ha ha ha! What say ye people? We have two Sheriff's Guards surrounded! Shall we put them in the stocks? Ha ha ha!"

Tami had apparently seen this coming, because she'd already taken the long way 'round and was waiting on line for drinks about fifty yards further down the path.

"Well... well met, Little John. We really just want to quaff some ales and watch a show. So..."

"Not until thou dost tell me the Secret Robin Hood's Merry Band Password! Ha ha ha! I shall give thee three guesses!"

Shelly stepped forward, smiled wide, exposing two ferocious fangs, and growled. Even the hair on the back of MY neck stood up. (And I've seen her naked.) Little John dropped his quarterstaff. "Why, that's it!" He bellowed, backpedaling out of our way. "The fair lady has gotten it in one! Huzzah!"

If you haven't been to a Renaissance Festival in a while, you might not recognize it. Twenty years ago, most of them were just temporary villages cobbled together by artists, role-players and hippies in an attempt to recreate the pageantry and "simple" lives of the European Renaissance. Now there's a Ren Faire in just about every county in America. Guests see open-air Shakespeare, jousting tournaments, beggars in mud pits, falconry shows and lots of wacky street performers juggling, fire-eating, singing, swashbuckling and some just making the same dumb jokes a thousand times a day. Thousands of part-time actors get to spend their summers playing great roles for ten hours straight: Sir Walter Raleigh. Sir Francis Drake. Lucrezia Borgia. Queen Elizabeth I. Robin Hood. And so on. Traditional artisans find an enthusiastic marketplace for their leatherwork, fantasy armor, pottery and patchouli. Then, after a few weeks, they pack it all up and move on to the next faire. I guess there's always been a kind of magic to it. For a few short weeks every year, there's a place where you can step through a doorway in time. You can see sports nobody's dumb enough to play anymore. (Even Knobs hasn't got the balls to ride a horse directly at a sharp stick. Jesus!) Eat food you can't get anywhere else. Well, actually, you can, but in the Renaissance, they couldn't afford silverware, so everything was apparently served on a stick. Steak on a Stick. Sausage on a Stick. Pork Chop on a Stick (pretty damn good, actually) and, I swear to God, Macaroni and Cheese on a Stick. Maybe they served that in Renaissance Canada.

But Ren Faires were always fun. Lots of fantasy. Nothing was real. Until the Purges. That's when we realized that some of our favorite Renaissance dead people were still walking around. Ertzbeth, for instance. Lucrezia Borgia. Thomas Howard, the 17th century Duke of Norfolk, who, two years ago, tried to lead a cavalry charge on Buckingham Palace to wrest the throne from Elizabeth II. Dumbass.

So now, Renaissance Amusements Limited™ licenses the names and likenesses of major living historical figures to Faires around the world. Faires that pride themselves on their authenticity hire architectural and fashion consultants who had actually lived in the buildings and died in the clothes. R.A.L. will even, for a significant fee, arrange guest appearances by actual Renaissance royalty. After dark, of course.

And that's the other difference you might notice. Today's Faire stays open a lot later —through the night in some places—to cater to the Nocturnal crowd. For some night-walkers, a Ren Faire is less fantasy than nostalgia. The Faires have become polarized, too. The daytime crowd is more family-friendly than ever, because the Goths and S&M types don't show up until sundown, when they come out to hang with their role models after dark.

By the time we'd worked our way around Little John, Tami had four cups of viscous yellow liquid set up at a picnic table near the edge of the woods..

"Tami, what did you buy us?" asked Knobs as we sat down.

"It's mead. It's like wine made out of honey. You'll like it."

"I'm really a beer guy. Not a big honey man either."

Shelly threw her arms around Knobs and squeezed. "Oh yes you are, my big honey man!"

"That's not…"

"Shut up. Give me some honey!" Knobs hugged her back and kissed her.

"What have we here? MEAD VIRGINS?" I looked and saw Peter Pan standing on a large rock just behind our table. "Ha ha ha! I be Robin Hood, fair ladies, and nothing pleaseth me like…"

"Uh, Robin?"

"Anon, Little John! I am about to introduce these fine folk to the sweet joys of mead!"

"Robin, methinks these folk wisheth to be left alone."

"And that is why we calleth ourselves Robin Hood's Merry

Band! Now where wert we?"

Little John leaned in and whispered into Robin Hood's ear. All I heard at the end was "Grrrrrr!" Robin gave Shelly a double-take. "Be that the cry of a peasant in distress? I must be off, good people!" He scrambled down from the rock.

Before he could run, "Wait!" I called. "Robin Hood!" He turned back, warily. "I need to find a certain show. Could you tell us where the Incredible Van Helsing Show is?"

"Certes, milord. Milord Maarten performs every hour on the half hour at the Cuckoo's Nest Stage."

"And where, pray tell, my lord, is that?" asked Tami.

"'Tis beyond the tourney lists, past the New Globe, bear ye right at Haypenny Path, pass the Mounds of Mayhem, a half-turn widdershins and thou shalt see it through the willow copse..."

"Could you just point?"

He leaned in conspiratorially. "Other side of the big lake. Listen for the screaming."

"Gotcha."

"But listen. I hear you've got a lycanthrope with you. 'Milady.'" He tipped his feathered cap at Shelly. "If you're here for the contest, you've got to wait until after dark."

"I don't know anything about a contest," said Shelly. "Knobs, are you setting me up for one of those wet T-shirt things?"

"Oh, no, Milady! That is the Soggy Bodice contest at the Varlet Stage, going on right now! If you run you might still get in..."

"No, that's quite alright."

"Shame, really."

"That's enough, Hood," said Knobs. "Tell us about this other contest."

"'Tis quite simple, in sooth. He fights vampires and lycanthropes."

"That's illegal!"

"Oh, not to the death! Bare handed."

Knobs and I responded almost simultaneously: "Oh, this I've gotta see."

We had a few hours to kill before sunset, so Tami, Knobs and I grabbed our drinks and we all set off to catch a few shows.

First up was the Living Nine Man Morris game. The last time I'd been to a Ren Faire the performers had played Living Chess. Giant chess board on the grass. Each piece represented by a player. And when a piece got taken, they fought over the square. "Pawn takes knight!" Hack, slash, parry, parry, "I yield!" Pawn takes the square! Fun. Lots of swordplay and, if you understood chess, the game was fun to follow as well. Then came the Purges, and wouldn't you know it, it turned out the court jester who had invented Living Chess for King Louis XII had gotten himself turned in 1545. He sued R.A.L. and won the trademark to Living Chess™. Some of the biggest Faires, like the city-sized spectacles in Texas and California, could afford the license. Not this one. Since I have no idea how to play Nine Man Morris, to me it looked like a bunch of people walking in circles and swiping at each other with swords and axes. The game was pointless. But the swiping was fun.

Tami dragged me off to see the joust. Three handsome guys (and one hot girl—welcome to the 21st century!) in armor, bashing each other with sharp sticks. Again, the sword-swiping was fun, but I'm not a big horse guy. So I dragged her off to see a bunch of busty wenches singing dirty—excuse me—"bawdy" songs.

We lost track of Shelly and Knobs for an hour or so. The last we saw of them, Knobs had tracked down a pint of dark red ale and Shelly was sipping from a water bottle. They were holding hands, heading toward something called the Kissing Bridge.

Then it was time to catch the daytime version of the Incredible Van Helsing Show. And incredible's a pretty good word for it. We got there just a few minutes before it started, and every seat was already taken. Now, when I say "seat" I mean hay bale. The stage was basically a twenty-foot long raised platform of two-by-sixes, backed by plywood that had been covered in textured paint to make it look like stucco. An arched doorway in the middle of the stage was covered with a satiny curtain. Overall, the stage had a vaguely Italian flavor to it. At one end stood a wall of thick boards. At the other, a pommel horse. The stage sat at the bottom of a slight downgrade. Hundreds of hay bales radiated out in a semi-circular arc. It gave the effect of an amphitheater. We were stuck standing in the back.

Knobs and Shelly sprinted up to us, Shelly flushed with excitement. She grabbed Tami, hugged her tight, and started whispering something in her ear, but her words were cut off by a high piercing note from behind the curtain.

It was the opening note of a beautiful gypsy tune, played on a violin. Played very well, if my tin ear is any judge. Two gypsy-styled drummers emerged from either side of the stage, one playing a squat ceramic doumbek, the other a car-door-sized frame drum called a tar. The curtain swept back and Van Helsing launched himself out onto the stage. He did a complete standing somersault without interrupting his tune, then leapt onto the pommel horse, performed a back flip onto the stage and finished the tune in a complete Russian split. Every woman in the audience, as well as a few of the men, started to scream. Even Tami and Shelly. And the show had just begun.

The description in Van Helsing's profile didn't do him justice. He was both more misshapen and more attractive than any of us could have expected. He wore loose, billowing crimson pants tied at the ankles; dark brown leather boots; a long loose-fitting brown leather vest festooned with knives; and a silk, collarless and sleeveless white shirt open at the throat. Even from thirty yards away I could see that his face sported a latticework of scars. One eye was nearly closed with keloids. His arms, as well, looked like old logs someone had taken a hatchet to. He was cadaverously thin for his height. His knuckles were knobby and swollen like an old arthritis victim. But he moved with the grace of a 16-year-old ballet dancer. Or more to the point, like an incomparable martial artist, which, it occurred to me, is exactly what he was.

The show progressed from feats of agility on the pommel horse to amazing whip tricks and then juggling, all accompanied by the exotic beat of doumbek and tar. He juggled six knives, four bowling balls and then, something I'd never seen, three birds. He juggled them upside down. That is, as each bird flew into the air, he coaxed them back down into an aerial cascade. Gorgeous. Finally, Van

Helsing called for a volunteer. A plump little redheaded woman of about thirty ran for the stage, almost tripping over her own tongue. He kissed her hand and asked her name. "Dorothy!" she answered, already gasping for breath. He gently guided her to the wooden wall. Then he threw knives at her. A lot of knives. First he outlined her body in large blades—the stock knife-thrower's trick. Then he casually walked over and asked if she was alright. The woman tightly nodded "yes."

"I can hear her heart racing from here," whispered Shelly.

He asked her if she wanted to stop. She squeaked "no."

He kissed Dorothy's hand again, placed it flat against the boards, fingers spread, and walked away. As he got half-way back to his starting point, he wheeled. A tiny dagger blossomed in his hand and soared across the stage, landing right between her middle and ring fingers. She squealed again. More blades blossomed and sailed across the stage. As he backed up to the far end of his playing space, the blades flew faster and faster. The drum beat accelerated. Small blades traced her hands. Larger blades pinned her knees. Occasionally, he'd pull more than one blade, and juggle them first, teasing his audience for a few seconds, then, 'Thunk!' And with each 'thunk' Dorothy'd let go a shriek or, increasingly, a gasp. From the looks on the faces of the women around me, Dorothy wasn't the only one totally turned on by the show. Finally, as the drums beat toward a crescendo, Van Helsing pulled a long bamboo tube from behind the curtain, dropped into his Russian split, put the blowgun to his lips, and fired. Dozens of tiny feathered needles blossomed all over Dorothy's body. I immediately thought Van Helsing had finally screwed up and actually shot his volunteer. But then I saw her convulse in laughter, and saw the miniscule needles fall one by one onto the stage. She shrieked and pranced away from the boards, her whole body spasming in excitement. I can't say for certain that it was an orgasm, but it sure as hell looked like one.

"Oh, I think I need a drink," said Tami.

"I need a cigarette," said Shelly. "And I don't smoke."

Both women headed toward the nearest pub, leaving Knobs and

me scratching our heads.

Knobs was the first to put the show in perspective. "That guy's fucking nuts. Did that woman just..."

"Yeah, I think she did. I'm not sure ours didn't. But I'm not going to ask. Forget how he works the crowd, Knobs. Tell me. You're the martial arts guy. How good is he?"

"He's really good. He's Saturday afternoon Kung Fu Theater good. He's Crouching Tiger Hidden Napalm good."

"That's bad."

"Only if he's really our guy."

"I really hope he's not our guy."

Somebody tapped me on the shoulder and handed me a hat filled with greenbacks, from singles to twenties. I pulled a five out of my pocket, dropped it in and passed it to Knobs.

"Nope. This was the mellow show. I'm saving my cash for the 'contest' tonight."

I passed the hat along. We waited for the crowd to disperse, then wandered off toward the nearest pub. I ordered two Octoberfests and two meads.

"None for me," said Shelly.

"OK. Hold it, please. One mead and a... water?" Shelly nodded.

"Being good today?" Tami asked.

"Being good for the next seven and a half months."

"What's happening in..." I started to ask.

Tami jumped and screamed so loudly our bartender spilt her mead and had to go pour another one. They hugged for what felt like a full minute. "Oh my goddess! Does Knobs know?"

"I'm standing right here, Tam." A grin like I've never seen on our young man split his face like a toothy canyon. I threw an arm around his shoulder and shook his hand.

"That's not all." Shelly held up her left hand to show us a single diamond flanked by two red stones.

Tami screamed and hugged our friend again.

"How long have you been wearing that?" I asked, incredulous.

"Nearly an hour, Mr. Detective." Shelly stuck her tongue at me.

"Since the Kissing Bridge," said Knobs. No tongue. "That's where I asked her."

"Is that silver?" I asked.

"Really? Really?" Shelly tilted her head and furrowed her brow at me like I was a typo.

"It's white gold, Brother," Knobs clarified. "I don't know jewelry, but I know what my fiancé is allergic to."

Tami came to my rescue with the next awkward question. "So is the…" she pointed to the ring, "sort of connected to the…" and made the universal big belly sign for pregnant.

Together they both blurted:

"She didn't know!"

"He didn't know!"

Knobs grabbed Shelly's face and kissed her hard and happy.

"Seriously," Shelly said, when Knobs let her up for air. "I just found out a few days ago and decided to wait to tell him today, at the world famous 'kissing bridge.'"

"And I've been carrying THAT around for about a month, waiting for the right time. Suddenly, we're on a kissing bridge, so…"

Sunset was a long time coming. Especially since Knobs and I had to keep our judgment sharp, but the girls didn't. That meant Tami knocked back a few meads while Knobs and I nursed one ale each for about three hours. Shelly stuck to water, but by dark, both girls were still giggly while Knobs and I still had work to do.

Finally, trumpets blared, and torches flared around the park. Candlelight bloomed in shop windows. Braziers lit up the courtyards. As a mild chill set in, the performers pulled out light wool cloaks. Deerskin jerkins. Fingerless gloves. Some of them left, bidding us stragglers "good 'den!" Time for the night shift. A few new performers strolled in. Graceful acrobats and barbaric warriors. All a little bit unearthly. A new line formed at the front gate. Hundreds of guests who'd waited until dark. Not all of the newcomers were Nocturnals in the scientific sense. Probably no more than ten percent, in fact. But they were all night owls in one way or the other. Here to party. Here to drink and cheer and strut their finest 'garb.' Mostly here to escape the real world and throw themselves into a fantasy. Just like the folks who were here all day. Same fantasy, just a shade darker.

We went back to find the Incredible Van Helsing Show—nighttime edition.

He wasn't in the little amphitheater anymore. We asked a passing black knight where the main man had gone. "Nine Man Morris board, Milord. Can't stage our fights in the dark so Maarten puts on real ones there."

Fights. I've got to admit, I was juiced about seeing it. I've only ever heard of one man taking on a nightwalker mano a mano, and it almost killed him. Knobs still has scars running down both thighs where he got raked with two-inch werewolf claws. Nocturnals are just too strong. Too fast. And they can see in the dark. And Van Helsing fights them every night?

This time we got to the stage early enough for front row seats. Good thing, too. This crowd dwarfed his daytime show. Two dozen torches ringed the Nine Man Morris board. At the far end stood a small pavilion. Curtains parted and Van Helsing stepped out. In spite of the chill, he was stripped to the waist and barefoot. His chest was striped with scars, including a pentagram carved into his right pec. He was missing a toe. We knew from his profile that he was only about 165 pounds. Spread out over a 6'6" frame, he looked like Olive Oyl's bad-ass brother. Off to the side, the drummers from his daytime show led a troupe of six more in a tribal rhythm. None of that "where's the downbeat?" drum circle shit, either. These guys were good. Van Helsing opened his fists and let drop two small balls on chains, which he began to swing in intricate patterns. As he danced with the spinning balls, he walked over to the torches. The balls passed through the flames and ignited. Now he spun like a dervish, cocooned in a glowing web of fire. The firelight gleamed on his sweat.

"Well, fuck me. He's doing a kata," said Knobs.

"Kata? Like a martial arts kata?"

"Yeah. Check out the kicks and blocks. He's doing it at a ridiculous speed, but it looks to me like a kung-fu kata. He's holding chains, so I can't see how his open hand-work is." As if he had heard the comment (and who knows, maybe he had; so far he'd lived up to the title "incredible") Van Helsing switched the right chain to his left hand and, still twirling, added an open-hand warm-up. Then, both chains shifted to his right hand, he warmed up the left. Finally, dripping with sweat, he let go of both chains so they soared across the board like comets, into a small bucket of sand near the pavilion. The drums cut off. He bowed and the crowd went crazy.

"Let me say again: I really hope this isn't our guy." I whispered to Knobs.

"My lords and ladies—nocturnal and diurnal! I, the Incredible Van Helsing, welcome you to The Pit!" Big cheer. "This is where we gather to settle old scores. Perhaps your grandfather devoured my uncle. Everyone's got to eat! And it's likely my great grandfather destroyed your grandsire! Staked him in his grave! Well, I say Grandpa was just doing his job. Am I right? Tomorrow bygones shall be bygones. The law is, after all, the law. But tonight? Oh, tonight you get a chance to take one last swing at the Incredible Van Helsing. And in the name of my father's father's father, I get to take a poke at you. Does that sound like entertainment?" Big cheer again. "Does that sound like excitement?" He cued the drums. They thundered a wild gypsy rhythm. "Well THAT sounds like a Call to the Brawl! Do we have a volunteer?"

Hands went up all around the ring. Too many of them were drunken normals with no clue what they'd be getting themselves into. Van Helsing ignored them. Finally, he spied a heavyset black guy with a unibrow, sitting a few yards away from us with some beer-goggled buddies, his hand half-raised.

"You, sir. Lycanthrope?"

His friends cheered. "Chewbacca! Do it! Take him DOWN!"

"Do you want to do this, sir? There's no pressure."

"I get pretty strong, and sometimes I lose it, you know? I don't want to hurt you."

"Don't worry about me, sir. Your name is...?"

"Robby."

One of his drunker friends called out "Chewbacca! Chew. Ba.

Ka! Chew. Ba. Ka!"

Van Helsing shut him up with a glare.

"It's just wrestling, right?" Robby asked.

"Or boxing. Fight however you like. Best of three falls."

"There a prize?"

"No sir, just the pride of winning."

"What the hell. I'm in."

"Excellent. If you'd like to go change out of your jeans..." He pointed to the pavilion.

"No, that's OK. I don't go all dog. I stay biped."

He took off his shirt. His chest hair was already sprouting. Muscles rippled and surged on his back. His face stretched, sprouted fur and became more muzzle-like. His fingers lengthened; his nails thickened into claws. He unsnapped a flap on the back of his jeans and a tail forced itself out. The change is different for everybody who undergoes it, but there are major classes. Some lycanthropes transform completely, like Shelly and Clawfoot, and some, like Robby, merely take on animal-like characteristics while retaining their human configuration. In lycanthrope circles, they're disparagingly called "furries."

Van Helsing took a neutral position at the far corner of the board. Robby turned to his crowd and howled, beating his chest like a gorilla. They hooted and chanted "Chewbacca! Chew. Ba. Ka! Chew. Ba. Ka!" Van Helsing just smiled, the scar over his eye crinkling the left side of his face.

From deep in his chest, Robby growled: "OK, let's go!" Claws tucked into his fists, he charged and swung a roundhouse punch. Van Helsing didn't even move his feet. His torso snaked out of the path of the punch. As Robby charged past, Van Helsing smoothly backhanded him on the shoulder blade, giving his upper body slightly more momentum than his feet. He tumbled.

"One fall for me," said the entertainer.

"No way. I tripped."

"Too easy!"

"Get a real fighter in there!"

Robby flipped his crowd the bird, which cracked them up. "Heh, no more running, I guess." He put both fists up like a prize fighter.

"Robby," said Van Helsing. "very nice of you to tuck your claws, but unnecessary. This is no holds barred."

"'S'OK. Looks like you got enough cuts on you already." Robby jabbed for Van Helsing's face which, of course, was nowhere near the fist anymore. The crowd started to jeer. "Pussy!" Robby punched again.

Van Helsing ducked and came up inside Robby's guard, hitting his furry gut with a double-jab-cross combination. Robby gasped and backed away. "Your claws, sir. You need them."

"No." Robby roared and started swinging like his fists were the flaming chains from the pre-show. Van Helsing smiled, ducked and weaved, danced away and jabbed, jabbed, jabbed, tagging Robby on the muzzle each time. The crowd was getting bored and pissed. "This sucks!" "You're not a wolf! You're a bitch!" "Get a fighter in there!"

Van Helsing's craggy left hand grabbed Robby's muzzle from underneath and squeezed, exposing the boy's fangs. He threw an elbow, scraping his own forearm across the canines. Blood sprayed. Van Helsing's blood. The crowd cheered. "What the fuck..." Robby began, but his opponent flipped him to the ground, hard, knocking the wind out of him.

"That was a fall, my friend."

"You see that?" Knobs asked.

"Sure did. Explain it to me later." Van Helsing dropped to a knee next to his foe and whispered in his ear. I leaned across Knobs. "Shelly, what's he saying?" She tilted an ear toward the chessboard, closed her eyes and concentrated.

"He's asking the kid if he's alright. Yeah, he's good. We have to put on a show, he says. Use your claws. You won't hurt me. Robby says no." Van Helsing grabbed Robby's paw and helped him up off the ground. He leaned in close.

"What's he saying now?"

"I'm sorry."

Van Helsing dropped into a sweep kick, which Robby avoided

easily, then leapt into a flying tiger, clocking the wolf-man right across the muzzle. Robby tumbled across the board, coming to rest in front of the crowd he came in with.

"Best of three," said Van Helsing. The winner raised his arms and accepted the cheers he'd earned, but he didn't look happy.

"Put your arms down! You're pathetic!" A middle-aged professor-type with an English accent stood up in the back of the crowd. A shock of red Einstein hair danced in the evening breeze above a light beige windbreaker, white jeans and a hellacious Hawaiian shirt. "I came to see the Incredible Van Helsing. All I see is a pathetic bully."

"And you are, sir?"

"My name is Riddleton. Saxby Riddleton. I fought your grandfather in 1927. He almost destroyed me, too! He was a Van Helsing! Not some circus freak."

"Well, Milord Saxby. Always a pleasure to meet an old friend of the family. My lords and ladies, would you see a battle?"

"What? I'm not here to fight!"

"Then shut up and sit down. Do we have any real men here?"

Before I could stop him, Knobs had his hand up.

"Lycanthrope or vampire, sir?"

"Neither. Human."

"I am sorry, I only fight nocturnals. Now you, Mr. Riddleton..."

"You asked if there were any real men out here," yelled Knobs. "I raised my hand. Why won't you fight me?"

The crowd, laughing at first, started to cheer for him. Tami's jaw dropped. Shelly seemed torn between concern for Knobs' sanity and pride in her Alpha.

"It was a figure of speech. See, Mr. Riddleton, for all your bluster, this mortal has got more balls than you have!"

"Damn you!" Riddleton spat. "You shall be my third Van Helsing, sir! I killed one of your Great Great Uncles during the Christmas Truce of 1914!"

"Doesn't that make you quite the douchebag? Why don't you come out here and we can all see the mighty douchebag fight?"

Knobs still wanted to test his stuff, but Riddleton v. Van Helsing promised to become a much better show than the humiliation of a young werewolf. So he sat down and watched. Studied, really.

As everybody now knows, vampires have a few decisive advantages in a fight against a human. First, they're often between three and five times stronger than the average guy. They're also terrifyingly fast. They can strike like cobras when they want to. Some of them cultivate claws, which are almost as sharp as their fangs. And of course, they're almost impervious to anything but silver, garlic, holy symbols or a chunk of wood in the heart. So unless you're holding onto one or more of these things, nobody in their right mind goes toe to toe with a vampire. Unless you're Van Helsing, apparently. He was out there empty-handed, stripped to the waist, about to take on—not just any vampire, but a pissed off cheater of a vampire—who claimed to have already killed at least one Van Helsing. During a ceasefire, no less.

I couldn't wait.

Riddleton pushed his way impatiently through the crowd, knocking people over right and left. He got to the front of the crowd and charged immediately. Van Helsing dodged, but Riddleton didn't rocket past as the werewolf had. Instead, he jabbed sideways, raking Van Helsing across the ribs. He pulled his hand back to find blood on his... yep, claws. Not many vampires these days shape and harden their nails into claws. Just the hardcore douchebags like this guy. He held his bloody claws up for us to see. The crowd roared. This was the fight they'd come to see! Then again, they were watching the vampire. Knobs and I were watching the vampire hunter. He was calm, smiling. Pleased.

Riddleton seemed to float around the field. Of course, he really couldn't fly, but his strength and grace cast the illusion of hovering. He circled the human, jabbing with his claws extended, trying to tear pieces of flesh. Van Helsing blocked and parried, but couldn't seem to land any blows. Riddleton got around behind Van Helsing and, taking advantage of the brief blind spot, reached to grab his neck. The move was so fast I doubt many in the crowd knew what was happening. Just as well, because it didn't work. By the time the hand got there, the neck was long gone. Van Helsing dove into a donkey kick and knocked the off-balance vampire right on his high and mighty ass. It had been a trap, and Riddleton had reached right into it.

"One!" bellowed Van Helsing, raising a finger in victory. The crowd bellowed back "One!"

Snarling, the vampire began slashing his claws like daggers. For all intents and purposes, that's what they were. Barehanded, Van Helsing turned aside each blow, blocking, parrying, keeping the sharp edges from his vulnerable veins. The combatants hardly moved their feet at all, but their arms were barely visible. As their velocity increased, making a complete blur of their hands and arms, the momentum abruptly froze. Riddleton staggered slightly, then yanked his arms back. But Van Helsing was holding on. He'd grabbed both of Riddleton's arms at the wrists. Van Helsing was no match in strength, but when Riddleton pulled his arms up, his foe followed, riding the vampire's momentum and sailing up over his head. Plummeting down into a somersault, he wrapped his ankles round the vampire's neck, and, using his own vampire-powered momentum, threw his opponent violently to the turf.

Leaping up, Van Helsing yelled "That's two!" and the crowd answered "Two!"

Van Helsing extended a hand to Riddleton, still sprawled on the turf. "Best of three falls, my friend. Thank you for an excellent fight."

"I'm not done yet! I'll rip your..."

"Chk chk!" and he stopped there, because three of the drummers were holding nocked crossbows aimed at his chest. Van Helsing, barely audible to the crowd, gave Riddleton excellent advice. "It was a good, fair fight. You lost. Go home." Then, bellowing, "A hand for Milord Saxby Riddleton! The finest combatant I have seen in ages! Give him a hand!"

Riddleton reluctantly bowed to the audience. He even gave up a grudging smile. As he reached the crowd, Robby the werewolf gave him a howl and a clap on the back. Riddleton grinned and took his hand. The crowd cheered some more.

"I'm next!" yelled Knobs, jumping from his seat.

Shelly, Tami and I hit him from three sides, tackling him into the pit between the rows of haybales. "Are you out of your fucking mind?" Shelly demanded.

"I can beat him."

"Did you watch the fight I just watched?"

"I can beat him."

"He just beat a werewolf..."

Without speaking a word, Knobs eyes said clearly, "I've beaten a werewolf."

"...and a vampire."

The three of us glowered at him, and he glowered right back. Ten seconds. Twenty. Now the crowd was starting to stare at us.

Knobs broke the silence. "I figured him out. Before this is over, you'll see. I can beat him. Now, if you won't let me fight, can I finally get drunk?"

Knobs and Shelly went off to get some hard (and soft) ciders. Tami and I headed for the pavilion to see if we could meet the incredible one himself. Two of the drummers were positioned outside the tent, ensuring the man some privacy. But I figured if he could stop by my house, I could barge into his tent.

"Excuse me. I was wondering if Mr. Van Helsing might have a few minutes to speak with me." Before they could object, I played my trump. "My name is Angus Wellstone." Sure I'm just a cop, but I'm a pretty famous cop.

"Never heard of you."

"Really?" I was crushed.

"Nah. Just shittin' you! You're the Twilight Cop. Nice to meet you. I'm Tristan. This is Gawain. Let me see if Maarten's cleaned up yet."

"Of course I am, and I am thrilled to meet the man who put me out of a job." The low tent flap opened, and all six feet six inches of Maarten Van Helsing unfolded from it like a cherry picker. He had his shirt on and was toweling off his damp close-cropped hair. He reached into the tent, pulled out the hat filled with bills, extracted a twenty and handed it to Tristan. "'Tan, please get me a beer, would you? And buy Gawain one as well." He pulled another twenty. "In fact, why don't you both go and bring some back for our guests."

"I'm fine, really..." I protested.

"We should talk," said our host.

"Sam Adams Octoberfest, if they've got it."

"You bet!" and off they ran.

'C'mon in." Stepping into Maarten's tent was like crossing into the twenty-first century again. While the outside was festooned with heraldic banners and ribbons, the inside was strictly business. A long workbench, piled high with neat piles of knives, swords, crossbow quarrels and other implements of destruction, dominated the twenty-by-twenty space. A power grinder was bolted to one end; a series of clamps to the other. Against one canvas wall stood an assortment of locked security cabinets. Across the room from the cabinets were a small flat-screen TV and a stereo. Four camp chairs encircled an electric camp cooler. Two Coleman propane lanterns lit the room to daylight brightness.

"I'm Angus Wellstone. I believe you've met my wife, Tami."

He shook my hand, then Tami's. "I don't believe I've had the pleasure."

"But you stopped by my house -"

Tami cut me off. "This isn't makeup." She held Van Helsing's hand in both of hers. "These are real."

"Of course they are. Angus, I've never been to your house."

Tami, still fascinated by the scars, said, "I thought they were part of the show, because when I met you last week..."

"Tami, we've never met."

"But he looked just like you! Except no scars. He said his name was Van Helsing. And he wanted to see Angus."

"My name is more common than you might expect. My face, on the other hand, and my height? Fairly unusual. And if he had no scars?" He gestured at his own face. "Then it was certainly not me."

"We'll get back to that mystery. When you invited us in, you said we should talk. Why?"

"I assumed you would have guessed. You know that it's all because of you that I work as a carnival sideshow? I was once the most sought-after killer in the world. I hunted vampires, werewolves, demons, rhakshasa. You name it. If it had fangs, I killed it. I was the best, you know. Ever. And I named my own price. Now everything I was trained to do—the profession I prepared for my entire life—is illegal. Because of you."

"And how're you feeling about all that?"

"I don't know." He got up and grabbed a knife from the workbench. I just about had to sit on my hands to keep from drawing my weapon. He started up the grinding wheel and worked a bright polished edge onto the blade. When he was done he wiped it with an oily rag and carefully stacked it with the others. He looked up at me from across the bench. "I don't know." Suddenly, he was around the bench and at my side. "But you wanted to talk to me, too. What can the Incredible Van Helsing do for the Wondrous Wellstone?"

"I just wanted to tell you how much I liked your show."

"Please don't bullshit me. You're not the fanboy type. You're a cop through and through. You're here on business. I haven't done anything illegal—at least not in your jurisdiction—lately—so I've got no problem talking to you."

I stepped between Van Helsing and Tami. I didn't like the way this was going down. Bad policy questioning a dangerous suspect without backup. Worse doing it around an innocent bystander. "Tami, please step outside."

"She can stay. I have nothing to hide."

"Tami, outside."

"Are you afraid I might hurt the Astonishing Thami?"

I barely had my weapon clear of the holster when Van Helsing kicked it across the tent. I'd like to kid myself that shoving Tami through the door while drawing my weapon slowed me down. But the fact was, I didn't stand a chance. He was just too goddamned fast for me. I threw myself at him, which actually caught him by surprise. He must have thought I was smarter than that. No sir. When my wife's involved, I'm as dumb as they come. In the small crowded tent, he didn't have a lot of mobility so I caught him with my shoulder and we both went down, taking the tall row of cabinets with us. As we both scrambled to get a superior position, I bellowed, "Where did you hear that? Who told you that name?"

But I was wasting my breath. He was focused on the battle. One second I was clawing my way out from under a cabinet, the next a steely arm had snaked around my throat. He pushed the back of my head with his other hand. We were still both sprawled on the ground. I started to black out. Then the pressure lifted. The arm slowly released me and I crawled away across the floor. I looked back to see an arm protruding through a rip in the canvas wall. At one end was Knobs. At the other was his Glock, the muzzle pressing up against Van Helsing's temple, pinning him to the floor.

"You OK, Angus?"

"I'm good, Knobs. Careful with him." I secured his arms with tactical restraints.

"What the hell are you doing? Get off me! I haven't done anything!"

"What are you doing, Angus?" Asked Tami from the doorway. "Why did you attack him?"

"Didn't you hear what he called you?"

"What?" Van Helsing asked. "The Astonishing Thami?"

I grabbed his restrains and pulled him to his feet. "Where did you hear that?"

"Ertzbeth Bathory!"

"That's right! Ertzbeth calls Tami that! Now how about you tell me how you know that?"

"I read Maxim!"

"What?"

"Maxim. The magazine. With the hotties on the cover. They did a 'Midnight Max' thing and interviewed Bathory. She talked about you guys. What, nobody told you about it?"

"We have it at home, Angus. She signed it."

"Oh, Christ. Listen, Van Helsing, this might be a total fuck up, but as long as I've got your attention I've got to ask you a few questions."

"Do I need a lawyer?"

"I'm way outside my jurisdiction right now. You don't have to answer a single question if you don't want to. But I'd really appreciate it if you would. In fact, let me cut those restraints off."

"You mean these?" He tossed the nylon straps on the workbench and sat down next to them. "Ask your questions."

"Have you ever met Ertzbeth Bathory?"

"No, sir. Haven't had the pleasure. Before the purges no one could afford the price to hunt her, and since the purges, I can't afford to date her."

"Funny guy."

"No. Seriously. A couple of hardcore spook hunters wanted me to track her down years ago, but Jesus—taking on the Blood Countess doesn't come cheap. Thanks to you, that's no longer an issue, so I'd just like to see her someday. Take her to the opera or something. She's… well, incredible!"

"Angus." A hand touched my shoulder. I jerked a little. "Chill, it's me," said Shelly. I hadn't even noticed her entering the tent. She pulled me toward the tent flap and whispered, "Angus, I'm no lie detector, but the wolf in me can usually hear and smell when somebody's afraid. Pheromones, sweat, pulse, you know? He was freaked when you went after him, but he's calm now. A little horny, actually, talking about Ertzbeth. I can't swear to it, but I think he's telling you the truth."

Never hurts to have the heightened sense of a werewolf around. Not admissible in court, but helpful on interviews. "Thanks, Shell." I turned my attention back to Van Helsing. "So you say you've never seen her?"

"No. Not in person."

"So you were no where near her penthouse three nights ago."

"I don't even know where her penthouse is." Van Helsing offered, "Maybe if you told me what you're looking for I could help you out."

"I can't do that. Let's just say somebody who can do what you do did it to some people we all care a lot about. And then somebody who looks like you do, minus the wear and tear, showed up at my house."

"I see. Conundrums wrapped in enigmas," Van Helsing gave a slight smirk.

"Wrapped in a body bag." The smirk disappeared. "You know,

some people think cops make Detective because they love mysteries. Conundrums. Enigmas. Just the opposite. We hate mysteries. That's why we try so hard to stomp the shit out of them. And I really despise this one. Listen, Maarten—I've been a bad guest. You've been pretty cooperative, given my behavior. I can tell you one thing: a lot of folks with thick folders full of facts think you're a very bad man. I can't prove you're not, so all I can suggest is 'don't leave town.' You don't want this getting all federal and manhunty."

"You know why I wanted to meet you, Wellstone?"

"No idea at all."

"Because I like it here. I really like this life! When it seemed there was no point to it anymore, I simply walked away from the family. No one has ever walked away from the Van Helsings. Yet no one even tried to stop me! That told me everything I needed to know: I was nothing anymore. But I wind up here, and it's a great life! What the hell is wrong with me? So I thought, maybe meeting you... well that would make me remember everything you cost me. I could fight you. Maybe kill you. Turn back time and be The Van Helsing again. Not The Incredible Van Helsing—this stupid parody of myself!" He paused and took a few deep breaths to ratchet the drama down a few notches. "But now I've met you," big grin, "and I don't feel any different about my life. I still like it here, and I don't want to kill you. Maybe I want to thank you. I don't know yet."

"Yeah, well, you let me know when you figure that out, OK?"

"You betcha."

"Hey! The lines were really long!" Tristan and Gawain piled into the tent carrying four beers each. "They were out of Sam. I got you Bass." They didn't even notice the chaos.

"Sorry guys. We were just leaving..."

Knobs cut me off. "Bass?"

Hell, we had time for one beer.

● ● ● ● ●

We left Van Helsing's tent at a little after 10 PM. Yes, we had more than one beer. Once you got past the scars, Maarten was a hell of a charmer.

We got back to town around 11 and walked down to the Bastard for another beer. We had the weekend off, right? Might as well enjoy it. We got a quiet table in a back corner and ordered a pitcher of Yeungling. I wanted to take our minds off the case for a little while, but Tami gnaws at mysteries just like I do. The talk turned to Peggy's killer as soon as the pitcher appeared. Tami's first comment floored me.

"I still think it's him," she said.

"Where'd that come from?" I asked. "An hour ago, I thought you were going to run away with him."

"Oh, I still might. He's hot, and talented —"

"And oh, so dangerous," Shelly added with a growl.

"Oh, yes," Tami agreed too enthusiastically. "But hot doesn't mean innocent. Who else could it be? He showed us he could do it. He told you he thought about doing it—but no one could afford him..."

"Actually, what he said was no one could afford it before the purges." Shelly corrected. "And after the purges it was illegal. That's not the same thing as saying 'No one can afford it,' or 'I would never do it.'"

"You said he was telling the truth!"

"It sounded and smelled like he was telling the truth. But maybe he's pathological. Some natural liars don't have any tells. And what, I've been a wolf six months...?"

"And you said the guy at the house didn't have scars," said Knobs. "Maarten's scars were not makeup."

"Maybe he wears makeup when he's out among the public," Tami suggested. It didn't seem likely that she wouldn't have noticed, but hey, I hadn't been there.

"But why stop at your house, then deny it?" asked Knobs.

"Maybe he had something planned and then changed his mind." I frowned, thinking of what he could have done to Tami if he'd wanted to. "I was going to say chickened out, but I don't think that's a factor. No, either there are two of them, or something changed his mind."

"We didn't get enough tonight to even bring him in," said Knobs.

"Angus, as long as we're working this together, how comfortable are you telling the ladies Lord B's story?"

No one could hear us in the bar. It's the first time I was happy Bar Voice Jay was there. His bellowing drowned out everything else.

Tami and Shelly, inquisitiveness notwithstanding, are not cops. As I've mentioned, Tami's a physical therapist. Shelly's our county coroner—paramedic by training. But if they hadn't both chosen the healing arts, they would have made kick-ass cops. Just between you and me, half the cases Knobs and I have closed, we owe to brainstorming with our ladies.

"I don't think B would mind." We huddled in close and I brought them up to speed on what we really knew about the case; why we were convinced it was a Van Helsing in the first place.

"OK, so Abraham Van Helsing never found Varney's fortune," Tami summarized, "but the family's got plenty of lucrative work to keep them in shiny sharp things. Until you, Knobs and Gustafson turn off the tap, permanently. Now no one will pay the last Van Helsing to do the only voodoo that Van Helsing's do so well."

"One last score?" suggested Shelly.

"The one that got away." Tami.

"Unfinished business." Knobs.

"Enough to retire on?" I asked. "Or is this a new line of business? Is he going after more of the long-lived, or is this one hunt his whole focus and then he's done?"

"Focus. Focus? Camera." Tami's a stream-of-consciousness brainstormer. "The camera's the focus."

"Keep going." I saw where she was headed, but saw no point in racing her there.

"If we can figure out why he took the camera, we can predict what he's going to do next."

Shelly looked puzzled. "How's that work?"

"It was random—off plan," Said Knobs. "It reveals more about his real desires than a well-executed plan."

"His plan was rational," I added. "People aren't. Unplanned acts are acts of passion, regardless how petty. And passion was the cornerstone of the plan. Figure out the passion and you know how and why the plan was built."

"Cool," said Tami. "You know, you're really hot when you get all CSI."

"Good to know. When we go home I'll start a fire and make some more shit up."

"Before you two get all forensic on each other, let's get back to the camera." Knobs ordered another pitcher. You've got to keep the brain lubricated in situations like this.

"What was he thinking?" I asked. "Go."

"She owes me." Shelly.

"Got to get something out of this." Knobs.

"Nothing at all. Instinct." Tami.

"I like that." Me. "Valuable. Portable. Mine. Keep going."

"Geez—Uh, What a stupid bitch. Owns all these cameras and she doesn't even show up on film." Shelly.

"Let's leave a red herring," Tami.

"I wonder if it's got film." Knobs.

"I got blood on it. Better take it." Tami.

"OK, anything ringing anybody's chimes?" I asked.

"I'm liking the instinct thing," said Knobs.

"Why's that?"

"Because he was able to get past her security, into the apartment, and all the way through to her bedside without waking her up. If he was there to burglarize the place, he would have grabbed more on the way through. Sure that one camera is valuable, but it's on par with a lot of the stuff in her place."

"I think Knobs is right," said Tami. "This guy's a taker, born and bred. He saw something valuable and just swiped it."

"What about the red herring theory?"

"Well, it's kind of moot, right?" asked Shelly. "If he took the camera to throw us off, then it's safe to work with the theory that there was no meaning to the theft. Same outcome, right?"

"Good point. So where does this leave us?"

"He's not done," said Knobs.

"You're sure?"

"He'll never be done. In the middle of carving a woman up, he makes the time for a petty theft. This is more than what he does. This is what he is."

"The worst part is," Shelly said, "Ertzbeth and Peggy were totally inconsequential. The treasure he's after, even the antique camera, are more real to him than the people who get in his way."

"So now I really hope it's not Maarten Van Helsing," I said.

"Why?" asked Tami.

"Because I sort of like him. And whoever we just profiled is a completely irredeemable monster. I don't want to think I'm that bad a judge of character."

12

On the Sabbath day, we rested. Well, pretty much.

Sunday is Gun Day. Weapons blessing day, that is.

"And what have we got today, officers? The usual?" Reverend Mossier—Rev to his friends—stepped around the pulpit. His congregation was still dispersing, waving and hugging goodbyes. Rev was the minister at the Unitarian Society of Hawthorne, and the hairiest son of a bitch I'd ever seen—not counting werewolves, of course.

"Nothing special today, Rev." Knobs hauled our "discreet" style weapon case out from the nursery. Rev doesn't believe in locking kids in a sound-proof room during service, so he lets us lock our weapons in there instead. Knobs laid the five-foot long soft-sided case across the backs of the rear-most pews, unlocked it and started unloading our gear, carefully placing each piece on the wooden bench. He unstrapped two schlager-bladed rapiers, two Smith & Wesson .45s, two Glock 36 subcompacts, a range of speedloaders, a jar of garlic juice, and my personal favorite, Xena—my silver-capped nightstick.

Rev picked up a sword and examined the paint-thin coating of silver running down its razor-sharp edge. "Lord, you have seen fit to fill our world with wondrous beings—cousins in the family of the Lord." He poured a few drops of water on a white cloth and rubbed down the length of the blade, then repeated the process with the next sword. He placed the swords back in the case. Knobs strapped them in. "You have granted us free will, and for this we praise you and pray for your guidance." He picked up the garlic juice, clearly labeled 'Concentrated Garlic Juice for Official Use Only' and made the sign of the cross over it. He popped the screw-on lid and we all recoiled slightly from the belligerent odor. "Give us the wisdom to do your will here on earth." He picked up Xena and smeared two fingers of the blessed garlic concentrate down the shaft. He then picked up the speedloaders and carefully dabbed each round—lead and hardened ebony—with water. "And, Lord, when we must use force to protect and serve your people, may we do so with right mind, clear heart and your blessing." Knobs and I finished strapping the weapons back into the case as Rev scrubbed the garlic oil off his hands with a Baby Wipe.

We'd been visiting Rev for the weapons ritual for about six months. Before that, it had been a hell of a long time since I'd stepped inside a church for more than a wedding, funeral or, since the Purges, a Holy Water pickup. I'd lapsed from the Catholic church in my twenties, not really having lost my faith, just my religion. I'd sort of gone into Do It Yourself mode, religion-wise, blessing my own weapons every night before I hit the streets. In fact, I still do. But one afternoon as I was picking up some Holy Water at St. Anthony's on Diamond Bridge Ave., Rev buttonholed me on the sidewalk.

"You don't actually attend this church anymore, do you Angus?" he asked.

"Nope. Just picking up." I shook the Holy Water bottle, then popped it back in my breast pocket.

"Oh, you don't go to church, but you count on Holy Water to keep you safe from vampires. Does that sound fair to you?"

"I don't farm, but I use garlic. Is that fair?"

"Not the same thing."

"It's worked so far, Rev," I'd said. "Whoever's up there juicing up the Holy Water seems O.K. with my M.O. I do believe, you know. I just don't attend."

"What do you believe?"

"Really, got all day? Ever seen Bull Durham?"

"Short version, then."

He clearly wasn't going to let me off the hook, and we did have a bit of history between us, so I thought about the question and gave it the most respectful answer I could come up with. "Rev, I believe in the prayers I say. I believe someone's listening. I believe in the sanctity of the oath I took as a police officer. And I believe in results. Nine out of ten vampires surveyed agree: my holy water does the trick. So Rev, I appreciate where you're going, I really do, but I try not to fix what's not broken." I mimed tipping my hat and stepped past him.

"Before you go," Crap. "Just one thought, Angus." I stopped. I really liked the guy, mostly because he almost always spoke sense, which is not something I can say about most of the clergy. So I surrendered and let him have his say. "Jesus of Nazareth never said one word about the police, guns, vampires, werewolves, holy water— none of it. All He ever asked of us was to 'Take this and eat. Do this in remembrance of me.' When that holy water burns on a vampire's flesh, and saves your ass, the Lord is doing you a major favor."

"And I appreciate it. That's why I say the prayer every night before I go out."

"But Jesus didn't ask for that. He asked you to stop by and have a piece of bread with his community. And to remember Him. That's all He wants. Stop by, eat with friends and, together, think of Him. Once a week."

"Sundays, right?"

"Yup. Same Christ time, same Christ channel."

"You're done before GameDay?"

"Always."

"I can bring Xena and her friends?" I shook the Holy Water again.

"We don't really stress the holy water thing in my congregation."

"You don't have to believe the same way I do. That's part of your theology, right?"

Rev grinned, shook my hand. "See you Sunday."

That's how we came up with Sunday is Gun Day. And that's how I started attending a Unitarian church. As a kid, I'd been told: 'Go to

Church or go to Hell.' Rev had been the first minister to invite me to church with a reason that didn't reek of brimstone: 'Come to church because Jesus asked you to.' Alright. Yeah. I guess He did. And the Rev had an interesting take on church. It's not all about God. It's about us. Break bread with the community and think about God. Listen, I'm no holy roller, but the first time I saw what holy water could do to a pissed off vampire, well, like the song says, "I'm a believer."

13

Sunday night confirmed our theory: our killer wasn't finished.

I was lighting some citronella torches out on the patio while Knobs wiped down the picnic table. Shelly and Tami were heating up some Moroccan chicken and flat bread. My phone rang. It was Commander Todd.

"Wellstone, I know you're not on duty tonight, but I think you're going to be interested in this."

"Shoot."

"There's been a staking. The suspect's on foot somewhere on Diamond Bridge Ave.."

"Who's been staked? You already have a suspect? Who?"

"We don't know yet, yes, and we don't know. Yet. But get this. He's tall. Real tall – maybe six-six and rail thin."

"Oh Jesus. Knobs, put the damn paper towels down. We think Van Helsing's staked someone right here in Hawthorne!"

"Is he fucking crazy?" Knobs ran to pick up the living room extension.

"Looks like it. Chief, who's out there?"

"McGinnis, Franco, Olanski and Pierowski."

"No! Not Pierowski!" Knobs yelled. "Where are they?"

"Diamond Bridge. The remains were left near the CVS and the

suspect was last seen on foot near the theater."

"Commander, we're two minutes away," said Knobs. "Get Pierowski out of there!" He hung up, grabbed his weapon and car keys. "Let's go." By 'go' he was out the front door. I hadn't even put my extension down yet.

• • • • •

INCIDENT REPORT
FILED BY OFFICER JAMES MCINNES HPD
DATE: SUNDAY, JULY 25TH 2004

At 20:15 hours Officers J McInnes and T Franco responded to an 11-27, suspicious person in the vicinity of the Hawthorne Movie Theater. Complaint lodged by theater manager, M. Toogood. Suspect described as "F---ing Ichabod Crane motherf---er." Officers asked for more helpful description and were told a man, roughly six and a half feet tall, extremely thin, was "creeping" around the back of the movie theater. Upon arrival in the alley behind the theater we discovered a charred wooden stake and organic remains consistent with the very recent destruction of an elder vampire. The ash and bones were warm.

Upon investigating the crime scene, Officers McInnes and Franco spotted an exceedingly tall man standing at the far end of an alley running perpendicular to Diamond Bridge Avenue. The man's right middle finger was running perpendicular to the rest of his closed fist. Officer Franco took umbrage at this and patiently explained that 'flipping off' an officer of the law constitutes criminal mischief. He explained this while running down the alley toward the suspect.

The suspect proceeded to pick up a garbage can lid and throw it down the alley like Captain America.

Officer Franco will require dental work but is expected to return to solid foods within two weeks.

Officer McInnes drew his weapon, ordered the suspect to freeze and called for backup and an ambulance for Officer Franco.

The suspect ran toward Diamond Bridge. Officer McInnes pursued.

•••••

TRANSCRIPT OF THE STATEMENT OF OFFICER MARGARET OLANSKI

TAKEN BY A. WELLSTONE AND D KNOBS, 23:25 HOURS, 25 JULY, 2004

A. WELLSTONE: Relax, Maggie. Just tell me everything you saw. Speak into the tape recorder.

M. OLANSKI: Well, Sergeant Pierowski and I were at the station when the call for backup came in. Clawfoot and I both grabbed our body armor and ran for a squad car. Diamond Bridge is just a few minutes from the station. When we turned off Lafayette, we saw McInnes running east on Diamond Bridge. And we saw this really tall guy running a few dozen yards ahead of him. Knobs, this guy was a freak. All leg. And he was fast! I swear we had trouble catching him in the car. But we passed him and cut him off. He was veering off into an alley until Clawfoot stepped out of the car. The guy saw Sarge and sort of backpedaled into this boxer's footwork routine.

A. WELLSTONE: What form was Sergeant Pierowski in?

M. OLANSKI: You kidding? When he heard Franco was down, his claws started to pop in the station! By the time we hit the movie theater, he barely fit in the car. And between you and me, JEEEEZUS does he smell when he changes. Anyway, he was almost all bear when he got out of the car. Good thing I was driving.

D. KNOBS: You said the suspect was moving like a boxer. Like he was looking for a fight?

M. OLANSKI: Oh, yeah! You kidding? If he was any more pumped for a brawl you would have heard the Rocky theme.

A. WELLSTONE: Where was McInnes during all this?

M. OLANSKI: He was running down the road toward us. He kept yelling 'Freeze!'

A. WELLSTONE: And how did that work out?

M. OLANSKI: You kidding? He might as well have been yelling

'Bonzai!' He got there as Pierowski took his first shot. You've seen Clawfoot's paws. They're the size of dinner plates. He swung one at this guy's head so fast I could barely see it. But the guy just ducked it like Clawfoot was in slow motion. So Clawfoot tries again. This time an upper cut. The guy fades back. Swoosh. Miss. But when he comes back in, he's got two of those little—they look like gardening tools—three spikes, the middle one really long?

D. KNOBS: Sais.

M. OLANSKI: That's it! Sais. Well, apparently sais matters—ha I kill me. Fuck, I shouldn't make jokes. I'm sorry.

A. WELLSTONE: It's OK, Maggie. It's natural. It's called black humor. When you've been a cop a couple of years you'll get used to it.

M. OLANSKI: Well it's just that the rest of the fight? It was all his. The sais must have had silver on them.

A. WELLSTONE: They did.

M. OLANSKI: Thought so! Clawfoot kept swinging, and he'd get stabbed in the paw every time. And roar! Just a poke. Swipe. Poke. Roar! The way he was cutting loose it sounded like his fur was on fire. McInnes and I were both trying to get a shot in, but the tall guy kept getting behind Clawfoot. Clawfoot was screaming. I mean screaming. There was blood pouring down his arms. His paws were smoking from the silver. Clawfoot went for a bear hug. Both arms, just grabbing. Tall guy got under the arms and just started pistoning the blades in and out. He was punching with them, stabbing stabbing stabbing. Oh fuck, Angus, Sarge was screaming so loud!

A. WELLSTONE: It's OK, Maggie. Oh kiddo, c'mere. Sarge will be alright. Turn that off, McInnes, will you?

J. McInnes: Not supposed to, Angus.

D. KNOBS: Turn. It. Off.

McInnes: I can't. Two cops are down. We have to do this right.

A. WELLSTONE: OK. Shhh. Shh.

[sound of chairs scraping.]

[thirty-five second silence]

A. WELLSTONE: You ready to tell us what happened next?

M. OLANSKI: Yeah. You swung in, Tarzan!

D. KNOBS: Tape's still running.

M. OLANSKI: You arrived on the scene, Detective Darius Knobs. You and Detective Angus Wellstone. Knobs, you were diving out of the car before it even came to a stop.

A. WELLSTONE: Yeah. Don't do that when you're driving, OK?

D. KNOBS: Sorry.

M. OLANSKI: Can I tell you, Knobs, you looked a little weird?

D. KNOBS: How, weird?

M. OLANSKI: You weren't moving like you. You move like lightning usually. But tonight you stalked over there like you were dragging roots.

D. KNOBS: Tell us what you saw.

M. OLANSKI: You stalked over, reached out, grabbed him by the back of his long neck and just held on. He kept twisting and slashing at your forearm but you kept him at arm's reach. How is your arm?

D. KNOBS: It's been through worse.

M. OLANSKI: Finally he dropped the sais and pulled a gun. That's when Angus shot him. Knocked him out of your grip but he got right back up. He pulled a little bottle of something out of his jacket and spilled it on Clawfoot's wounds. Clawfoot started to smoke and scream some more, and that's when the guy got away.

A. WELLSTONE: Thank you, Officer Olanski. You did good tonight. We'll get the guy who hurt Clawfoot. Damnit, McInnes. Now you can turn it off!

• • • • •

I felt bad for Maggie. She worships Sergeant Clawfoot Pierowski and she felt like she really let him down. The only thing she did wrong was think like a daywalker. She hesitated to shoot for fear of hurting a fellow officer. A more experienced overnighter would have known better. She's got a weapon on her hip loaded with nothing but lead. She could have shot Pierowski right in the eye and barely pissed him off. But that half-ounce of lead would have slowed down our killer, Kevlar or no Kevlar. At least it would have gotten him away from Clawfoot for a few moments. Maggie's young, so I gave her a pass. McInnes, on the other hand, got an earful. He made the same mistake but he's been at it a lot longer. As for Knobs, hell knows what he was up to.

"What the fuck were you thinking?" Once again, Knobs and I found ourselves in the chapel at Valley Hospital. It was a good place to have a friendly professional chat about the night's events. "You could have gotten yourself fucking killed! You know how good that son of a bitch is!"

"I can take him."

"You were just standing there letting him stab you!"

"I was winning."

"Great. What's the trophy, a five foot chunk of granite that says 'Here lies Darius Knobs. He was a winner when he wasn't trying to commit suicide?'"

"He barely touched me." He held up his bandaged arm. To tell the truth, I'd seen Knobs hurt worse. "Sais are stabbing weapons. They suck for slashing. I had him. Maarten was mine."

"If it was Marlten at all."

Only one person I know would pronounce 'Maarten' as 'Marlten.'

"Ertzbeth!" She stood in the doorway, leaning jauntily on a cane. She was dressed in black silk pajamas, Chinese slippers and a red silk robe. I couldn't see her face at first, because she stood silhouetted by the light from the corridor. As she stepped into the chapel, she averted her eyes, slipped the robe from her shoulders and gestured at the cross. I took the robe and draped it over the icon. She finally looked up and I saw her face. Though it was almost completely healed, I could easily make out where she'd been cut. The patches of newly regenerated skin were fairer than the rest, nearly white, in fact. He eyelids were perfect, but her eyelashes had not come back. And her usually lush red lips were blue, cyanotic.

"You have not yet caught the killer of my Peggy."

"We will."

"I know you will. Two reasons. First, you promised me. That is enough. I do not need a second. But we have two nonetheless. The second reason is that I am now helping you."

"Ertzbeth..."

"And you will try to talk me out of it..."

"Ertzbeth."

"But this happened to me. And to my Peggy. And so I will be there when Van Helsing pays."

"Ertzbeth, you have to..."

"My body will have time to heal when my heart has been healed."

"Ertzbeth!"

"What?"

"You have to get dressed. I'm not driving you around town dressed like FrankenGeisha. And we've got a call with Lord B in fifteen minutes. I want you on it."

"Oh. I will go dress. Wait here."

• • • • •

2 AM. The phone was ringing as we walked into the conference room. Before Todd or McInnes could get up, I reached across and hit 'handsfree.' We could all hear. I glanced at the caller ID. "Morning, B. We've got me, the Commander, Knobs, McInnes and Miss Patchwork Quilt of 1576."

"The Countess is up and about? Wonderful! Welcome back the land of the unliving, my dear."

"'Tis good to be back, you beautiful little man."

"Thank you for letting me listen in on your briefing, Commander Todd," said B. "It appears your local incident earlier this evening is directly related to the attack on The Lady Bathory and dear Miss O'Farrel. Angus, I believe you have the floor this morning?"

"You've all read the preliminary statements from Olanski, McInnes and Franco. And Knobs and I were both there to confirm the description of the attacker. It's Van Helsing."

"Did you see his face?"

"I didn't need to see his face," said Knobs. "His fighting style was unmistakable."

"Check out Mr. Miyagi over here," said Jimmy McInnes. "Whack on. Whack off." He picked up two pens like chopsticks and mimed plucking flies from the air. Knobs snatched one of the pens from his grasp and impaled a real fly on the conference table. McInnes put the other pen down.

"Fighting styles aside—although I do agree with Knobs—this guy moves just like Maarten," I said, "we've also got motive and opportunity. McInnes, you take it."

"The victim's corpus was largely reduced to ash, but there was no obvious sign of any kind of accelerant," he began, referring to his notes. "Also, his clothing, while scorched, mostly survived intact. Both factors suggest that the victim was most likely an old to elder vampire. Personal items that survived the immolation include a gold crown—"

"A crown? I assume you mean the kind used to cap a tooth?" asked Commander Todd.

"That's what it says here, Chief."

"Do vampires get dental work?" Todd pursued the question. "I thought their bodies healed perfectly."

"It is possible," said Ertzbeth, "likely, in fact, that this vampire had such rotted teeth before death that the transformation had no effect on them. Scars, tattoos, and such, have been known to remain after a turning."

"Do we know if the crown was put on during his lifetime, or afterwards?"

"Sorry, Commander," said McInnes. "Not yet. County forensics is still sorting through ash. I just about had to threaten to marry the tech's daughter to get this much this soon. There was only one other item. A piece of steel jewelry, round, about 12 grams, found in the crotch of the man's pants. The coroner says he has no idea what it is."

"Ha!" snorted Lord B. "The bugger had a Prince Albert!"

"We're learning so much here tonight," I mused. "Knobs is now a sensei, and Lord B is a connoisseur of crotch jewelry."

"Would anyone care to explain to the unwashed masses what exactly, a Prince Albert is?" asked Todd.

"It's a very English thing," B began. "Or, at least, it was. Prince

Albert, or so rumor has it, was inordinately endowed. Born in Germany, he tried his best to be a proper English gentleman. And so, concerned about presenting a proper public profile, he took measures to ensure that nothing got... out of control... to spoil the line of his trousers."

"I have no idea what you are talking about," said Todd.

"He pierced his pecker and pinned it to his pants leg."

"Oh, my God!"

"Word got out. 'Prince Alberts' became all the rage in the 1850s."

Todd shook her head as if to shake the image out through her ears. "Victorian England? Genital piercings were all the rage? You're making this up."

"No Commander, I assure you, I am not. In fact, I remember the first time I laid eyes on Queen Victoria, I was almost moved to cut my own member clean off."

Franco chimed in. "With respect, Mr. Ruthven, that's an urban legend. The Prince Albert was developed in the 1970s by an artist in West Hollywood."

"With respect as well... Franco, is it? Hard to tell on these damned speakerphones. Whom would you rather trust? Snopes dot com or an eyewitness?"

"Eyewitness?" asked Franco.

"You have read my poetry, Mr. Franco?"

"Well, I've been meaning to get to..."

"Never mind. Let me say this: I can vouch for the veracity of the 'urban legend'... first hand."

Commander Todd ended the discussion. "Well, I think we will defer to Mr. Ruthven's greater experience in this matter."

"I do apologize for the digression, Commander," said B. "Let us get back to the subject of evidence. If he was pierced, he was likely pierced before death; otherwise the hole would keep healing and you'd have found the bauble in his sock. If he had had bad teeth as well as a Prince Albert during life, we can assume he was English. Anything else, Officer McInnes?"

"No. No wallet. No watch. No money. Nothing."

"What was he wearing when he died?"

"Khaki slacks, a windbreaker and a godawful Hawaiian shirt."

"Riddleton!" said Knobs.

"Bingo," I confirmed. Then I explained for everyone who had not been quaffing ale with us on Saturday, "We saw Maarten Van Helsing fight Saxby Riddleton on Saturday night. It was an invitational challenge thing. Van Helsing won, and they shook hands, but I think Riddleton went away angry. He could have come back..."

"Or Van Helsing could have tracked him down later to rob him," finished Todd. "Mr. Ruthven, has your organization got a file on a Saxby Riddleton?"

"Unless he is living as a renegade, which I doubt, we have him on file." Lord B's side of the call went silent for a few moments. A few keyboard taps, the whirr of a hard drive. "Yes, here we are. Let me e-mail this file to you. Directly to Angus, and a copy to you, Commander?"

"That's fine." Over the open speakerphone we heard more hunt-and peck typing, then a "whoosh."

"It's sent. You should have it momentarily."

My iPhone buzzed, so I headed for my office to print out a hard copy. As I left I heard McInnes ask, "E-mail must seem weird to you, huh, Mr. Ruthven?"

"How so?"

"Well, messages were sent by horse and carriage when you were..." And that's all I heard. I turned on my computer, logged in, downloaded my e-mails, found B's message and printed it. When I got back to the conference room, B was still answering the question.

"...images soaring through the air on radio waves. Whole cities immolated by the unimaginable power of the atom. Satellites orbiting miles above the earth bearing spy scopes that can count the hairs on my very head. Men playing golf on the surface of the moon. Unmanned vehicles exploring the surface of Europa. Diseases eradicated by decrypting and altering the very code of existence. Vampires and men sitting down for a drink... of scotch. No, Mr. McInnes, e-mail does not impress me much. But if I ever get vertigo from Googling I shall be

THE OVERNIGHT: BLOOD FOR THE MARKED MAN

thankful for your concern."

McInnes whispered, "No one told me he was so touchy."

"I've got your file, B. Bear with me as I share it with everyone else."

"Certainly."

• • • • •

NOCTURNAL PROFILE
Name: Riddleton, Saxby, II (Colonel)
Designation: Vampire (Old)
Born: June 12, 1828, London, England
Turned: August 30, 1878, Kandahar, Afghanistan
Current Residence: Sugar Loaf, NY, USA

Military History Pre-Mortem
Crimean War 1853 - 1855 - British Navy
2nd Afghan War - 1878/79 Kandahar Field Force (under Lt-Gen Donald Stewart); (Turned at Kandahar)
Military History Post-Mortem
Zulu War - No 1 Column Roarke's Drift (AKA Chancey Ridley)
Battle of the Transvaal - 1890 (AKA Chancey Ridley)
1899 Imperial Yeomanry, South Africa, 1899 - 1902, awarded the Queen's South Africa Medal (AKA Jason Connery)
The War of the Mad Mullah - Somalia - 1903 (AKA Jason Connery)
World War I - Ypres Salient 1914 - (AKA Saxby Riddleton III)

• • • • •

"And it goes on and on. He's got medals from every major Western conflict since the Crimean War, right through to Vietnam. Everything from the Purple Heart to the Victoria Cross."

"So the guy's a hero?" asked McInnes.

"It would appear so," said Lord B. "He selflessly fought for humans. And how is he repaid? A stake through the heart from the mortal 'champion,' Van Helsing."

"George Gordon Noel!" Erzbeth snapped, like the world's hottest librarian. "You know better. Tell the whole story and stop misleading your allies!"

"How dare you!"

Ertzbeth barely whispered, "No," leaning across the table so her cyanotic new lips almost brushed the speakerphone. "How do you dare? For years, decades, we put up with your ridiculous 'Victor Ruthven, Lord B' nonsense when everyone knows exactly who you are. Why do we do that? Do not interrupt. We do that because we are your friends. Your allies. Yet you seem determined that your colleagues—your friends, Victor—shall hunt down this very formidable Van Helsing person, be he guilty or no. I will now tell them the truth of the Old Guard—so we all know what kind of creature was destroyed last night. Then you will tell me why you are so eager to destroy Van Helsing."

Awkward.

Ertzbeth paused the briefest moment, offering a window through which B could slip an apology or a protest. Neither came, so Ertzbeth turned to us. She placed both hands palms up on the conference table as if turning over playing cards. "This Riddleton may have been a member of a group known as 'The Old Guard.' They were a company of nocturnals who served in the British Foreign Service. Prince Albert certainly knew of them. Chinese Gordon. Napier."

"Yes, yes," B cut in. "British vampires have fought for the Empire as far back as Wellington. What has that got to do with anything?"

"You called him a hero. And you did not gag upon the word. Well done, Director Ruthven." Ertzbeth pushed the speakerphone away like it was a dish of roasted garlic. "Angus, Commander, if Riddleton was Old Guard, as it appears he was, know this: He traveled with the army for but one reason: to feed at leisure and disguise his cast-offs as the carnage of war. All while military and political leaders looked the other way." She leaned back toward the phone with a grimace. "Old Guard? Heroes, Victor? A Wampyr facing nothing but lead bullets and iron bayonettes? Do not make me laugh. You know better. Now tell us. Why are you so convinced we are dealing with this Van Helsing?"

"Wait wait wait," interrupted Todd. "I don't care about the Boer War or the Battle of the Bulge..."

"That was WW II, Chief," corrected McInnes.

"Shut up, McInnes."

"Yes, Commander."

Todd tapped the table with her thick brown index finger. "We have a crime scene report." Thud. "Three witnesses describe the same person." Two fingers. Thud. Thud. "And now we've got a motivating connection between the victim and the suspect." Thudthudthud. "Now somebody please tell me—and I am talking to you, Mr. Ruthven, since I think we are on the same page here—how many six-and-a-half foot-tall anorexic ninjas do we have to interview before we just go and arrest Maarten Van Helsing?"

"None, Commander," said Lord B. "I, for one, am convinced he is our man."

"Then we are all in agreement." Erztbeth began to object but Todd cut her off. "Everyone who is here in an official capacity agrees. Tomorrow I will ask the court to issue an arrest warrant. Angus, Knobs, if you want in on the arrest, you'd better go home and get some sleep. We're doing this one in daylight. Thank you, Director Ruthen, we'll be in touch when Van Helsing is in custody."

Todd reached for the phone to end the call, but B's voice interrupted her. "Commander, since this case remains under BNA jurisdiction, I will be sending some of my own people to assist."

"Fine by me." She thudded the speakerphone button hard enough to jam it, rose and walked out, without a glance at Ertzbeth or myself.

14

I'd managed almost six hours sleep before the phone rang. Todd had the warrant. She told us we were expected to rendezvous with B's team at a Park and Ride lot on Route 17, about two miles from the Renaissance Faire. After a quick stop at the station to pick up the paperwork, Knobs and I headed north.

We pulled in around 10 AM. The Park and Ride is nothing more than a huge parking lot for commuters riding the Metro North railroad into New York City. It being a Monday, the place was packed with hundreds of vehicles. We circled the lot twice. Just as I was realizing this might not have been the smartest place to rendezvous with a team I'd never met, a black Dodge Sprinter cargo van at the far end of the lot flashed its lights. The van was wedged between a canary yellow Hummer and a cherry red Ford 250 pickup, so we just parked crosswise in front of it. The passenger side panel door slid open, scraping the paint on the Hummer, and three men climbed out, leaving more scrapes on the Hummer's roof and hood. The driver's door opened a few inches, dinged the Ford and slammed shut again. The window rolled down and a woman climbed out, dropping into the Ford truckbed. She vaulted over the tailgate to the asphalt.

All four were dressed head to toe in white, gray and black urban camo tactical gear. Their boots looked like they were designed to walk on the moon. They had more pockets on their pants than I have in my whole wardrobe. Their t-shirts, made out of some kind of thick spandex, highlighted every muscle. And they were armed for a siege, with three Heckler & Koch MP5 compact submachine guns and a 23 pound M60 7.62mm machine gun. That's in addition to whatever else they had crammed into all those damned pockets. None of them were wearing any kind of military or police insignia. There was no way to tell who was in charge.

The driver approached. Six feet tall, blond, breasts the size of my head and triceps almost as big. She put out her hand. "Detective Wellstone, I'm..."

"Before you even introduce yourself, I want all those automatic weapons locked back up in this rolling arsenal of yours."

"This is standard procedure, Detective."

"Put them away or we roll out of here empty-handed and you can tell Mr. Ruthven he's no longer welcome to Thanksgiving dinner at Chez Wellstone."

"Wellstone, I don't know who you think you are..."

"I'm the guy with the warrant. You want to barge into an amusement park with machine guns on your hips, you go right ahead. But you do it without a warrant. And you know what? I don't see any ID on any of you. Put the weapons down right now or I call the State Police and we go all Waco on your anonymous asses. How do you want it?"

The nameless driver considered for a moment, then signaled the others to do as I'd said. They looked at the van. Then at the Hummer and the Ford 250. Back at the van. One of the men sighed, climbed back over the Hummer, scratching the hell out of the roof again, and slid open the van's side door, ripping another three-foot scratch down the Hummer's passenger side. Piece by piece, his friends handed over their automatic weaponry. It took a while. Once everything ridiculous had been safely stowed, I stuck out my hand. "Angus Wellstone. This is Knobs. Welcome to my case."

"Now you're done pissing a circle around my van you want to be friends?"

"That's right."

She smiled. A big lush mouth filled with big white teeth. Like upside-down tombstones. "Fair enough. I'm Angela Michealo. I run this unit." She introduced each of her men. "Ricky Kestler." Another muscular six-footer, head shaved, with a little black patch of hair under his lip. I hate that look. "Ginno Reilly." Little guy with thick black hair and an Irish accent. Slim and squirmy. He never stopped moving. "And Antar Boulad." A giant Arab. He was wearing a shamag and ogal (yes, I had to look them up), the traditional headscarf, and had prayer beads tucked into his web belt. He was the guy who had been carrying the M60 like a rifle.

"What is this unit?" asked Knobs. "Who are you guys?"

"We're Noc 1, a special ops unit of the BNA. Designed and trained to handle some of the newer challenges of our post-Purge world."

Reilly chimed in: "We're the Brothers Grim!"

"Not the real Brothers Grimm," clarified Kestler.

"We just call ourselves that," said Reilly "'cause our job is grim and we're all like brothers!"

"And they wouldn't let us call ourselves the Grim Reapers," added Kestler.

I looked to Boulad to see if he had anything to add. "I don't even get the joke," he said.

"I don't get this whole set-up," said Knobs. "You're trained to take down nocturnals. Van Helsing's one of us. What the hell are you guys doing here?"

"Mr. Ruthven thought you could use our help," said Michealo.

"Van Helsing's a lot tougher than he looks!" added Kestler.

"And how would you know that?" I asked.

"Who do you think trained us?" asked Reilly, casually spilling beans that I'm pretty sure were meant to be spilt.

"Shut up, Reilly!"

"Oh let him talk, Michealo," said Kestler, "but do it in the van. I want to get this over with." Knobs took Boulad and Kestler in my car; I rode with Michealo and Reilly in the Grim Go-Cart, as Reilly called it. (I made Michealo pull it out of the spot first.) Grim is right. The whole van reeked of WD-40, Tiger Balm muscle ointment and cordite.

During the five-minute ride to the faire site, I got the sound-bite version of the Brothers Grim from Michaelo. They'd been brought together a little over six months earlier by Lord B himself, which suggested to me that they were the BNA's reaction to last year's little demon adventure in Hawthorne. The one that had almost gotten all of us killed. The team comprised two Navy Seals (Michaelo and Kestler), a London Special Branch anti-terrorist agent (Reilly) and one Lebanese Marine Commando (Boulad). B brought in the very best instructors he could find. And that meant working with the greatest of all vampire hunters: Van Helsing. It was finally starting to make sense. Why was B convinced Van Helsing was the killer? Because he'd seen him in action. Why was he so personally caught up in the case? Because he felt responsible for Maarten's actions. Maybe he was responsible. I didn't know enough yet. But I would.

The faire is only open on weekends so that Monday morning we arrived at what appeared to be a nice, quiet half-deserted English village. I insisted we play nice, so Michealo, Reilly and I stopped at the main business office and asked the receptionist where we could find Mr. Van Helsing. She was the very spirit of twenty-something blond perky helpfulness and didn't even bat an eyelash at the paramilitary getups on the Brothers Grim. I think if we'd been dressed as Klingons she would have sold us season passes. She told us that The Incredible Van Helsing camped during the week in his performance tent behind the Chess Board, but that we couldn't go on site without an escort, so if we would just stay put for a few minutes she'd call the security supervisor and he'd be here in a minute and could she get us some coffee while we waited? And before I could stop her, she was on the radio calling a guy named Ned to the office. She'd barely put the radio back into its cradle when three middle-aged guys with paunches the size of beer kegs burst through two doors, handguns drawn. At a glance, the weapons looked like police-issue 9mms. And these guys were holding them properly. I pegged them all for retired cops.

"Put your hands where I can see them! Jeannie, get out of here. Hands up!" Hands over my head, I glanced out the window and saw three police cars pulling in, lights flashing, but no sirens. Knobs, Kesler and Boulad were standing outside the van, also with their hands up.

One of the security guys, a big redhead, kicked Reilly's legs apart and began to frisk him. Reilly wheeled around, knocked the gun to the ground and backhanded the guy. Before Reilly could get another punch in, I grabbed a handful of his thick greasy hair and bounced his head off the receptionist's desk. As he collapsed on the office floor, I put my hands back up.

"Very sorry about that. Please do not shoot my stupid friend."

"Who the fuck are you?" asked the redhead.

Michaelo started to answer, "This is a classified…"

"Jesus Christ shut up! Listen, my name is Angus Wellstone. You must be Ned." The redhead nodded. "I'm a detective from New Jersey on loan to the Bureau of Nocturnal Affairs. Can I reach in my pocket and show you my badge?" He nodded. "Thanks. I'm here with a warrant for Maarten Van Helsing. These two are Whoop and Ass, just in case Van Helsing resists and we have to open up a can."

Red looked over the badge and the warrant and finally put his weapon away. So did the other two. He picked up the radio and told his men in the lot to stand down, too. "Of course I've heard of you, Detective Wellstone."

"Call me Angus."

"Mind if I give you a little tip, Angus? Next time you bring a swat team to somebody else's sandbox, pick up the phone first. Knowamean?"

"Understood, Ned. Think I can get your help in serving this warrant?"

"What'd you have in mind? Frankly, I like Maarten and I don't relish putting cuffs on him. Especially in front of the other rennies. Rennies – folk who work the faire. Then again, I also don't want to catch one of his knives in my teeth."

"All I need is for you to watch the perimeter for us. This is a huge site and we don't know it at all. If he runs, we could lose him pretty easily without your men on radio."

"That I can do."

•••••

We stayed in our two teams and crossed the faire site on foot. Working the treeline for cover, we skirted the jousting field, where a few of the stunt riders were working their horses. We passed the main shopping area, mostly deserted except for some shopkeepers doing maintenance on the gardens around their booths. From the gestures and comments tossed our way, I got the impression that artists who work the Renaissance Faire circuit are not big fans of authority. That's all right. I wouldn't welcome black ops teams creeping through my backyard, either. I just smiled, waved and kept creeping.

It took about ten minutes to get to the Nine Man Morris board. Michaelo, Reilly and I approached Van Helsing's tent while Knobs, Boulad and Kestler hung back under cover of the trees. A few yards from the tent, I signaled Michaelo and Reilly to hold back, too. I did a quick pat down of my body armor to make sure everything was shipshape. Chest. Crotch. All good. Nothing on the head, neck, arms or legs, unfortunately. Nothing to be done about it now. But I kept picturing Van Helsing throwing those daggers and wished I could borrow some plate mail from the joust team.

I drew my Sig Sauer 290 9mm. I chose it for this mission for a few specific reasons. It's small, has a half-cock mechanism you don't often find on semi-automatics, and it's got a custom wooden grip that makes it really hard to drop. That was the clincher. I'd already lost one gun to this guy's flying feet.

"Maarten? Maarten Van Helsing?"

"That you, Wellstone?"

"Yes it is."

"C'mon in!"

"Maarten, I'd rather you came out. With your hands over your head, if you please."

"What the hell is this?"

"I have a warrant and you have until the count of three." I pulled a butterfly knife and flipped it open.

"A warrant for what?"

"One."

"I haven't done..."

"Two."

"...anything."

"Three."

I stepped away from the door and slashed the side of the tent open with the knife at the very moment Van Helsing slashed the door itself. I had him in my sights through the rent canvas as he faced the wrong way with a dagger in each hand. My weapon was half cocked, a round already in the chamber and the trigger half depressed. "Go ahead, ninjaman, try something kicky."

He laughed. "What a great move! I'm going to use that someday. But I'll give you credit."

"Not unless you can slash through steel bars. Michaelo. Reilly. Move in. I've got him. Maarten Van Helsing, you have the right to remain silent and refuse to answer questions. Anything you do say may be used against you in a court of law."

"Save your breath."

"You have the right to consult an attorney before speaking to the police and to have an attorney present during questioning."

As Michaelo reached through the slit in the door to cuff Van Helsing, he grabbed her wrist and pulled her through. The move was so sudden I almost squeezed off the shot. To avoid shooting the woman, I pointed the muzzle at the ground. Good thing I did, too, because the next thing I knew, Reilly came sailing over the tent and his scrawny frame hit me like a 150 pound bag full of bowling pins. We both went down, and my chambered shot went off into the tent floor. I scrambled to my feet, stepping all over Reilly, I'm afraid, and spotted Van Helsing running across the Nine Man Morris board.

Kestler was closest. He fired a shot just as a group of three horses and riders rounded a bend in the path through the trees. The shot missed its target but panicked the mounts. All three started bucking, and one reared and threw its rider, a young girl, to the ground. Boulad fired, too. He was set to full automatic, the bastard. The two other horses, wild and confused, bolted right at Kestler. Kestler turned and took aim at the lead horse. Van Helsing, almost under cover of the woods, turned and noticed what was happening behind him. He stopped, drew and threw, impaling Kestler's shooting hand. Kestler screamed as the horse ran him over.

Knobs checked on the thrown girl. She was stunned but conscious. He signaled Boulad to get her out of harm's way and grabbed the reins of her rearing horse. Muscling it under control, he leapt on and rode after Van Helsing. As he passed me all I heard was "...damned clusterfuck."

I grabbed my radio and called for Ned and site security. "He's running. Heading for the north end of the park."

"10-4. I've got three men at that end. If we see him you'll be the second one to know."

Great. Thirty-five acres and they've got three men.

"Demonslayer, come back. This is Alphamale"

"This is Demonslayer. Go Alphamale."

"Angus, he got away."

"Damn it!"

Michaelo was listening in. "Demonslayer and Alphamale? Tell me you didn't pick your own callsigns."

"What happened, Alphamale?"

"He's too goddamned fast. I had him outrun with the horse, so he dove off into thicker undergrowth. I had to dismount and just couldn't catch up. I'm sorry, Angus."

"Not your fault, Buddy. My bad planning. Come on back. He's long gone."

As I clipped the radio back on my belt, Michaelo asked, "So, you want to tell me who that guy was?"

"What guy?"

"The guy you chased out of the tent. Next time you want to go off-mission, give me a heads-up first."

"What the hell are you talking about? That was Maarten Van Helsing."

"No it wasn't. Sure it looked a lot like him, but unless he had an industrial accident in the last few weeks, that was not our instructor."

"Wait a minute. Your instructor was that tall, right?"

"Sure. There are lots of tall guys around."

"Skinny?"

"Yeah. Hey, they look a lot alike! I'll give you that. But Maarten Van Helsing is, well, he's cute. Your guy looked like a kitchen cutting board on legs."

"Lord B's profile said he had scars all over his body."

"I never saw a profile. But I met the man. I worked with him for six months. B could drown himself in profiles and still not know what he's talking about because he never met the man himself."

"B hired him and never met him?"

"How could he? Van Helsing only trains during the day. He says it's the only way to make sure he's training diurnals. He doesn't want any nocturnals learning his techniques."

"So there are two Maarten Van Helsings. Or at least two men calling themselves that name. And one of them is a sadistic killer."

"Or both."

"Or both. Crap."

"And don't forget they're both masters of more than a dozen martial arts."

"I haven't forgotten."

"And they know you're after them."

"You can shut up any time now, Michaelo."

For nearly four years, I'd considered Victor Ruthven, Lord B, a friend. We'd met working on the Twilight Treaty. At first, I'd pegged him as a dandy—a prancing clotheshorse who considered himself better than anyone else. That's the persona that sells the fashions so it's the one he shows the public. But behind closed doors the real Lord B took off the velvet cape, rolled up his oh, so puffy sleeves and dug in to the hardcore politics of forging a treaty that would end up saving countless lives. During the months we worked on the Treaty I watched him arm-twist, compromise, threaten, cajole, demand and sacrifice.

He also listened. To me. He asked tough, intimate, questions and actually listened to the answers. "What is it you daywalkers feel?" he'd asked. "How can we help you quell the fear? What does it mean to you to have your nightmares dragged out from under the bed?"

I'd had a few questions, too: "What does it mean to you that humans are no longer prey? Some day soon we won't be afraid of any of you, any more. Can you handle that?" We talked for hours. Honestly. Openly. We might have started out a little like Snoopy and the Red Baron, but we came to really respect each other.

I won't say we're 'buddies' or 'bro's.' B isn't the kind you invite over for poker and beer. But I was convinced that if there was one guy I'd trust to get my back almost as much as I trusted Knobs, Lord B was that guy. Trust between ancient enemies is very, very rare. And so hard won. But I had trusted B with my life. With Tami's life.

Suddenly, I wasn't so sure. Our friendship had been built on a kind of fearless honesty. I'm convinced he'd never lied to me before. Embellished, sure. He's a poet. But never lied. Never held anything back. Lying would have been a violation of himself. So what the hell was he doing with this case? What did he know that he didn't trust me to know?

He was holding something back. That made him a different man than the one I trusted, and it was putting me, and Knobs, and maybe even Tami and Shelly, at risk. And I had had enough of it.

I grabbed Knobs as he walked the horse back into the clearing. "Find a squire to take care of that. We're going to D.C."

15

We didn't stop to change or disarm. We didn't tell the Brother's Fuck Up where we were going. We just grabbed a sack of burgers and Pepsis at the Vince Lombardi Rest Stop and drove right through the day into the dusk. I wanted to get there by the time Lord B awoke, but we hit traffic outside Philly. We pulled up at the Bureau of Nocturnal Affairs offices at 7:35 PM. It was dark.

The BNA had recently taken over The Castle on the National Mall from the cash-strapped Smithsonian Institution. I'm sure somebody thought its Gothic mix of red sandstone towers and archways would make the nocturnal employees feel at home. B called it "kitschy."

We had to show our badges and check our weapons at the main entrance. No real surprise. But it only took me a minute to convince the officer on duty at the front desk that we had an appointment. He'd heard our names so many times around the Bureau I thought he was going to salute me. He let us upstairs without even calling ahead. Good.

We weren't quite so lucky when we got to B's office. He was, after all, the Co-Director of the Bureau, and shared a wing with ex-President Jimmy Carter. Security was a little bit tighter. I stepped off the elevator and approached the senior assistant's desk. "Hey, Candy. I've got an appointment with Director Ruthven."

"Hi, Angus. No you don't."

"Aren't you going to check your book?"

"I'd know." If I had to describe Candace Diamond, and I guess I might as well, I'd describe her as "efficient." Not just good at her job. Which she is. I mean efficient physically, and maybe even spiritually. She's quite thin but not bony. She keeps her dirty blond hair cut straight just above the shoulders and clipped back, and her nails perfectly manicured but short. That day she wore a simple blue shift that seemed to say, "Yes I have breasts but no, you are not invited to admire them." Everything on or around her desk rested within the radius of her reach. Sitting up straight and eyeing both the elevator and the emergency exit staircase with the rhythm of a security camera, she could reach anything in her professional universe—including the security phone, which she reached for immediately.

"Candy, it's me, Angus. Lord B in?"

"Security, Detective Wellstone does not have an appointment. Please show him the door until he makes one."

"Candy!"

Knobs was already headed for B's office when two BNA agents barreled in through the emergency exit. "Freeze!" Knobs is no dummy. He froze.

"Candy, we need to see Lord B. Right now. It's about a case. Buzz him and let him know we're here."

Serenely calm, as if telling us nothing more important than the code to the men's washroom, Candy explained, "Director Ruthven left instructions he was not to be disturbed. If he were expecting you, he would have let me know. Since you have never just shown up before without an appointment, I believe I can safely assume this is a surprise visit. Director Ruthven despises surprises. Gentlemen," she nodded to the security agents "Please escort the detectives to the lobby. From there they can call and make an appointment for a later date. Ta, Angus."

A door opened on the far side of the waiting area. "What is the ruckus, Miss Diamond?" A tall man with thinning white hair, liver spots, a cardigan and tweed suit jacket stepped through.

"Director Carter! I am terribly sorry if we've disturbed you. These gentlemen were just leaving."

"Mr. Wellstone! Mr. Knobs! Good to see you!" He extended his hand.

"Always good to see you, Mister President," I said, shaking hands with my favorite living ex-president.

"Mister President." Knobs came back across the foyer and shook hands as well. "You're looking good. How's Mrs. Carter?"

"Rosalynn is in excellent health. Thank you for asking. Now what, Miss Diamond, is the trouble here?"

"These gentlemen wish to see Director Ruthven but they do not have an appointment."

"I see. And we do enjoy standing on protocol. Tell me, Miss Diamond. Do I need an appointment to see Director Ruthven?"

"Why no, sir, Mister Director."

"Well then I see a way to split this log without anybody getting splinters. Miss Diamond, please announce me to Director Ruthven and I will bring my guests in with me."

"But Mister Director, Lord Ruthven was very specific..."

"As was Ah, Miss Diamond. Now please do me the courtesy of pushing that little red button by your right hand, or shall Ah reach over and do so myself?"

"No need, Sir." She pressed the button.

"Yes, Miss Diamond?" Lord B sounded groggy. He had probably slept through the day in his office.

"Director Carter and..."

Carter hushed her with a finger over his lips.

"Carter and whom?" asked B.

"Director Carter to see you, sir."

"Of course, please send him in."

Candy pressed a button under her desk. We heard the "chukt" of sliding deadbolts followed by the short "whoosh" of a heavy oak door sliding on carpet. Across the room, the door marked "Director Ruthven, Bureau of Nocturnal Affairs" slid partially open.

"To the vault, my friends," said Carter with a playful flourish, as he led the way.

We passed through the first door, which was about three inches thick and lined with a thin layer of steel. I no longer wondered where Ertzbeth had found her security contractor. Inside was a short foyer blocked by another, simpler door. Carter casually knocked.

"Come in, Jim! How can I... you are not alone." We were still in the corridor. Lord B had either smelled or heard us. He was on his feet and opening a cabinet behind his desk before we even passed through the doorway. As we stepped around the President, I saw—and heard—Lord B chamber a round in a Remington 12-gauge.

"What in the name of our sweet savior are you doing, Victor?" said Carter in his slow, soft Georgia drawl.

B swung the barrel away from the door, unchambered the round and put the shotgun down on his desk.

"Expecting somebody else?" Knobs asked.

"As a matter of fact, yes, I was. My apologies, Jim. Things have been a bit tense of late."

"Ah should say so. May Ah ask how you got the blunderbuss through security?"

"I had a number of surprises built into the furniture before we took over these offices. No one thinks to pass a bookcase through a metal detector. I hope this does not compromise our working relationship."

"Course not. Stop by my office some afternoon—sorry, evening—and Ah'll show you the new Beretta over-and-under ultralight. Buy me a soft drink and Ah might tell you how Ah got it in. In the meantime, Victor, perhaps you'd like to pull up a log and tell us a story. A story about assassins, Ah think. And vampires. Oooh, Ah cannot resist a good bone tingler. Can you boys?"

"No, sir," I agreed.

"Nothing better," said Knobs.

"Well there you have it, Victor. An eager audience. And a tale too long untold. Since Ah know this story already, Ah will leave you three to spin out your yarn at your leisure. Victor, Ah do advise you to be open with these men. We have a saying down south. Secrets are like socks. The longer you hold off airing them out, the worse they stink when you finally do."

"An interesting metaphor, but good advice. May I ask, Jim, how you know the story I am about to tell?"

"Not all U.S. Presidents ignore their intelligence briefings, Victor. Ah'm going home. Angus, Knobs, please carry mah regards to your beloveds."

"And you as well, Mr. President."

"Good night."

B's office was furnished with deep red leather armchairs and a black leather sofa. We all sat silently. And sat. B looked at everything but me. He even looked to Knobs for support, but Knobs might as well have been carved out of ice. I'd never seen B like this. Finally, he leaned forward, put his elbows on his knees and said, "Angus, four years ago I ordered your assassination. Now the man I hired to kill you works for me right here in the Bureau."

"Well I've got to tell you, seeing as I'm still sitting here, I'd fire the guy. He sucks."

"I wish that were the case. No, I am afraid your assassin is one of the very best in the world."

"And again, I point out the obvious. Four years later, I am still alive. Am I that hard to kill? Hold on a second. I'm doing the math here. Four years ago, we were still mortal enemies, right?"

"Yes, just barely. I ordered the assassination the morning of November 16th, 2000."

"That's the morning of the armistice," said Knobs.

B nodded.

I shook my head. "You ordered me killed in the morning knowing you were going to surrender that night? What the fuck good would that have done?"

"Our surrender was no sure thing until the moment it became a done thing. Angus, not all the nightwalkers were in favor of the armistice. Many wanted to keep fighting. Many believed we would all be destroyed if we let up for a moment. You own the day, when we are helpless. We saw the armistice as suicide."

Knobs interrupted. "'We?' You opposed the armistice, too? I thought you were all gung-ho."

"No. I was afraid. Terribly afraid. But Jefferson convinced me to conquer my terror of the true death and dare to do the right thing. I was not the only nightwalker trembling on the inside that evening in New York City. Of course, I had even more to fear than the rest. Before Jefferson gained my support, I had already made a deal with the devil and there was no backing out."

Knobs was incredulous. "You're saying you stood there in the U.N. Plaza under a flag of truce, knowing there was an assassin out hunting for Angus. And you didn't say anything."

"Not just Angus. You as well. Tami. And Shelly."

Knobs launched himself across the room and tackled B right out of his chair. He lifted the elder Wampyr by the throat and slammed him against the wall. B didn't fight back. I didn't move to stop him, either. "You sent a hired killer after our WOMEN?" Slam! "Shelly?" Slam! "Tami?" Slam! "What kind of monster are you?"

"Was I."

Knobs pivoted and drove Lord B face-first through the top of his desk. SLAM! "What?"

"Was I." Knobs hauled him upright. B spoke very slowly and very softly. "The proper question is, what kind of monster was I? If you will stop smashing my furniture with my head for a moment I will answer that question."

Knobs held B aloft for nearly 30 seconds. B waited, silently, not struggling or showing any resistance to the humiliating position in which he was held. Knobs finally lowered the Director to his feet and turned away. He walked to the far end of the room and stood, his arms folded, challenging B to make it good.

"What kind of monster was I? I was a vampire. A drinker of blood. A parasite. Long had I tried to best my hunger, to live in peace with the daywalkers, and I had succeeded. I thrived on animal blood for decades, with just enough human essence to keep me sane—every drop of it freely offered by my lovers. I had found redemption. I was the Wampyr who lived and loved as a man. But then your people started to kill us. None of us were safe. Even my little play coven of East Village fashion victims—all harmless daywalkers! Children! Were attacked by Christian Crusaders. They burned my shop. Killed my lovers. Hounded me underground. So I joined in the Reckonings. For months, I fought alongside my fellow nightwalkers. And do not fool yourself. All the 'heroes' of the Armistice fought, first. We fought hard. We sued for peace because we had to. Not because we trusted you. If we have grown to love any daywalkers since then—and we have. We have. It is as much a surprise to us as it is to you."

Knobs stood stone still by the door, but the tension had drained from his forearms and neck. I got up and helped myself to a scotch. About to put the bottle down, I took in B and Knobs, and poured two more. "Go on, B."

"The children I had loved were gone. Massacred. The life I had built, destroyed. And suddenly these lunatics—Jefferson and his dreamers—were trying to convince me to throw my fate to the mercy of the same slobbering mob that had butchered my dreams. I was afraid. And I was angry. But mostly I was afraid. I knew of a man. A man who would do anything for money. I had barely survived his ancestor's treachery. I sent word to Maarten Van Helsing."

"Holy mother of mayhem."

"Wait! Wait wait," said the suddenly animated Knobs. "Van Helsing hunts vampires! You sent him after humans?"

"I hinted that you had all been compromised. All it took was a hint. I don't think he even believed me. But it gave him a pretext. Permission, so to speak, to collect his bounty in what passes for good conscience among Van Helsings."

"And why us?" I asked.

"A symbol. Revenge. Lack of any other ideas. Call it anything you like. I blamed you. Many of us did—still do, as you well know. Your death seemed like a wonderful idea at the time."

"I received a call that night," I recalled. "Warning me to stay barricaded indoors. A woman's voice. Was she sent by you, B?"

"No. I wish she had been. When I discovered that you had survived long enough to meet with us at the U.N., I assumed that

Van Helsing had failed and forfeited his bounty. When I met you, I realized immediately what a terrible mistake I had made. I am not, for obvious reasons, a praying man. But over the coming months I offered thanks, to whatever deity would stoop to accept the prayers of a monster, that you had all survived my despicable plan. I was appointed to this undeservedly lofty position and dedicated myself to using it as a pulpit from which to foster brotherhood between our people. Then Van Helsing's people contacted me."

"His 'people'? As in I'll have my people get in touch with your people and we'll do murder?" asked Knobs.

"Exactly. I learned that Van Helsing is not simply a person, but a corporate family not unlike la Cosa Nostra. In the generations since the first vampire-hunting professor Van Helsing, the family had grown quite comfortable, leeching off the booty to be won ridding towns of their local nightlife. The clan raised and trained a number of expert enforcers, each known to the world as the "Van Helsing." Maarten is such an enforcer. And like la Cosa Nostra, the Van Helsing family has certain inviolable rules. The foremost of which is this: A contract is indissoluble. Apparently, over the years, too many clients have balked at the violent means by which the Van Helsings pursue their business. Therefore no Van Helsing contract can be broken. Ever. Once hired, a Van Helsing will fulfill his contract and he will collect, in full. I, of course, did not know this. I understand few clients do until it is too late."

"OK, but that was four years ago. Why hasn't anyone come after us since then?" I asked.

"Because I have kept Maarten Van Helsing busy."

"Busy? Dare I ask?" I dared ask.

"The contract cannot be broken, but it can be delayed. By offering Maarten continuous employment in a series of lucrative, but non-lethal tasks, I have managed to postpone the inevitable. Since I intend to outlive him by at least a few hundred years, I felt this was the smartest way to save your lives. Keep him working until he expires of old age."

I was still confused. "Then why's he suddenly gone rogue?"

B finally lifted the scotch I'd poured him. "Maarten's last assignment was to train Noc 1." He shot it back.

"The Brothers Grim?" Knobs asked.

"I hate that name. Yes. The Brothers Dim. Van Helsing has been training them for six months. He concluded that he could teach them no more and unilaterally ended the assignment."

"He taught them everything he knows in six months?" I couldn't believe it.

"No! By no means!" Ruthven waved the empty glass. Knobs and I both ignored it, so he got up and poured himself, and us, refills. "According to the terse note Van Helsing sent me, he taught them everything they had the capacity to learn. He claimed his services beyond that point were an insult to his training and expertise. So he quit my employ. And I have not received a message from him since."

"You said 'note' and 'message,'" I said. "Is that how you communicate with him? By mail?"

"The Van Helsings also have strict rules about employer-employee relationships. All the control resides with the employee. They never show their faces to the people paying the bills. I have never seen Maarten Van Helsing."

"Then where the hell did you get the gruesome description in your profile?" Knobs asked, almost shouting.

"We carefully interviewed a number of young ladies who have had intimate contact with him during his engagements on the Renaissance Faire circuit."

"That's pretty clever," Knobs conceded.

"Thank you."

Knobs leaned forward and tapped his finger on Lord B's brocade vested chest. "Except that they were fucking a different Van Helsing than the one who's been fucking you!"

B brushed Knobs' hand away. "A different Van Helsing? How can that be? How many six-foot-six Maarten Van Helsing's can there be?"

"Obviously at least two," I said. "Your own idiot squad said the guy we chased all over Sterling Forest wasn't their instructor.

And you just told us the family keeps a number of enforcers. Maybe they're brothers."

B mulled it over silently for a long time. I got up and dropped some ice in my scotch. Finally, B came to terms with the new intel. "So you are suggesting that all this time—four years—I thought I had your assassin under my watchful eye, when, in fact, I was watching the wrong man entirely."

"Sure looks like it." It's not often I get to make an elder vampire feel stupid. In spite of the context, it's actually kind of fun. So I pushed a little harder. "It never occurred to you that a Renaissance Faire performer might have a hard time getting away for combat training?"

"I was assured the Incredible Van Helsing show was purely part-time." even as he said it he dismissed it with a grimace.

Knobs brought us back to the problem at hand. "So all this—the contract, Noc 1— this is why you wanted us to go after the guy so badly?"

"I needed him eliminated. To protect you. And Tami and Shelly. And you two are the most resourceful agents for this kind of job."

Knobs clearly wasn't satisfied. "I still don't get why you'd send us right into the sights of the guy who wants to kill us."

"A situation like this is like shooting an arrow in the high wind. You can never hit your target shooting across the wind. Your only hope is to shoot directly into it. You two are my arrows. Only by aiming you directly at the threat could I hope that your keenness would carry you through."

"You know I hate when you go all Yoda on me, right?" said Knobs.

"Of course I do. Friends we are?"

"Friends we are."

16

We needed to find out more about this rogue Van Helsing. Since B's official connections had been an epic bust, Ertzbeth offered the assistance of her own spy network. Although I'd never dreamed she had a personal spy network, I found the news surprisingly unsurprising. Only the fact that it included mortals with access to Interpol files caught me just a little bit off guard.

Ertzbeth put us in contact with a communications engineer from Interpol, some programming genius in charge of implementing I-24/7, the round-the-clock international police communications network. He was a compact Frenchman, about 5 foot 8, somewhere between 25 and 30 years old. Since we picked him up outside the baggage claim at the Air France terminal at Newark Airport at 2 in the afternoon, I also knew he wasn't a vampire. He introduced himself as Jean Vidocq.

"You are friends of Mademoiselle Bathory?"

Knobs and I introduced ourselves and helped him get his bags to my car. I got right down to business. "Ertzbeth says you've got information on the Van Helsing family."

"Oui, the Van Helsing enterprise has been a subject of Interpol scrutiny for many years—even before the Purges. Of course, in those days we believed they were an international confidence ring. Little did we suspect their outrageous claims were true."

"We need everything you've got on Maarten Van Helsing," said Knobs.

"Non, that you already have. You need help with Martin Van Helsing." I know I looked confused. Knobs looked pissed. We both thought Vidocq was screwing with us. "Say it with me: Maaaaartehn." A long European roll of the tongue. "Martin." Flat. Midwest United States. "Maartehn. Martin. One is Dutch. The other, English. American to be precise. Your scar-faced troubadour is who you know him to be: the former enforcer for the European branch of the Van Helsing cabal. His American cousin, Martin, six years his junior, was attached to the American branch. We believe both men received precisely the same training. It appears to be a franchise thing — like how you cook the 'amburgers at McDonald's. Precisely the same tout le monde. But the American branch, it was never activated. Too many guns, too much competition. Not enough old world superstition, no viable market. In fact, we believe the Home Office was about to call the entire American team home to the Netherlands when the news broke about the werewolf in your hometown. Martin had already been training in Amsterdam as a backup for his cousin. Seeing an opportunity, the family expedited his instruction and sent him back to his home in the United States. He was prepared to execute the first Van Helsing assignment here in North America on November 16th, 2000. The Armistice changed his plans."

"Do you know who that first assignment was?" I asked.

"Non, On that, the grapevine, it is silent."

"Us. And our wives."

"C'est vrai?!" He sat back and looked us over, apparently trying to decide if we were ghosts or just the luckiest sons of bitches on the planet. "But you still live! C'est impossible!"

"Well now you see our problem. And why we need to know everything we can about the American branch of Clan Van Helsing. I'll set you up at my house. You can give us the whole download there."

• • • • •

"Vidocq. I know that name from somewhere." Tami had just gotten home from work, and was setting up the espresso maker.

"Perhaps you have heard of my ancestor, the master detective Eugene Francois Vidocq."

"That's it! Didn't he invent the whole concept of 'private' detectives?"

"Sorry, Tam," said Knobs. "That was the Pinkertons."

"No, she's right, Knobs," I said. "Vidocq launched le Bureau de Renseignements in Paris twenty years before Pinkerton caught his first man in Chicago." Jean winced as I butchered the pronunciation. Tough shit. He should hear himself say hamburger. "In fact, Vidocq built the French Surete, introducing the whole concept of "detectives" to Europe."

"I am deeply impressed, Monsieur Wellstone. I had been led to believe most of les Americains had no interest in European history. You, monsieur, are quite the scholar."

"I believe it's important that detectives know something of our own history. The masters of our craft can teach us a lot. And if we're going to follow in the footsteps of greatness, we should at least know where the great have walked."

"Very well said, monsieur. Tres bien!"

I didn't know Le Surete from Le Cirque de Soleil. I'd had Ertzbeth brief me on Vidocq's history before Knobs and I set out for the airport. Vidocq didn't have to know that. If he was any good he'd figure it out for himself. Based on his pedigree, I figured he was probably damned good. Eugene Francois Vidocq, Jean's direct ancestor, hadn't just been the world's first detective. He'd also been the fearless lunatic who'd rescued Ertzbeth and Lord B on the dock at Torre Annunziata. If this kid had inherited half his ancestor's brains and balls, he'd be running Interpol in a few years.

And that would be fine with Ertzbeth, I'm sure. Over the decades she'd maintained a close, mutually profitable relationship with le Bureau de Renseignements, Eugene Vidocq's private detective agency. That long relationship formed the core of what she now termed her "network." The same relationship also put Jean Vidocq in mortal danger. Martin was looking for descendants of the Varney conspirators, and I now had one sitting right in my living room. As if I needed another target painted on my house. In a strange way, though, Vidocq's presence was comforting. Sure, Van Helsing wanted us dead. But he needed to keep Vidocq alive for torture and interrogation. That meant as long as Jean Vidocq was in my living room, I didn't have to worry about arson, bombing or a drive-by.

I didn't say it was a great comfort.

Ertzbeth arrived at the house shortly after dark. She hugged us all emphatically, saluting Vidocq with a double cheek kiss. She looked infinitely better, no longer leaning on a cane, her skin tone restored to its uniform pearly blush. But only the shell was repaired. When she wrapped her arms around my shoulders, I felt the tiniest tremble. She held me a second too long and when she pulled away, her unearthly gold-flecked eyes were wet and clouded. She brought word from the hospital about Clawfoot Pierowski.

"Your friend, the giant bear, he has been in Intensive Care for three days. But he will not be as fortunate as I have been. His wounds have been closed. With great speed and great skill. By the same doctors who cared for me. All but one, and I fear his absence has made a terrible difference. Dr. Weintraub, who plucked the poison from my wounds, could not be reached in time. The doctors had not known to clear all the silver particles out first."

"Would there have even been time?" Knobs asked. "Clawfoot was bleeding out fast. Ertzbeth, it took Weintraub hours to clear your wounds. With no blood in the way."

Ertzbeth unconsciously ran her tongue over her new lips. "I remember."

"Sorry," Knobs whispered.

"No, you are right, my friend. The doctors may not have had any choices. But this will become a problem. A problem as large as Clawfoot himself. Lycanthropes, they differ from us, the Wampyr, as much as they differ from you. Lycanthropes do not die to become.

Their blood flows through their veins just like yours. Once the mighty giant's wounds were closed, Van Helsing's silver dust had nowhere to go but deeper into the body."

"The doctors shared all this with you?" I asked.

"I am very persuasive," said Ertzbeth, "but no. The sergeant's room was next to mine. I have very good hearing and have had nothing else to do but watch my own flesh regenerate."

"Eww," said Tami.

"Exactly. There is good news. The doctors, they are certain Sergeant Pierowski will live."

"And the bad news?" I asked.

"They say he should never change back to human form. They fear the trauma will kill him. Even as a Kodiak bear, the silver will most likely settle in his joints and ache like—what is it makes Commander Todd limp in the rain?"

"Rheumatoid arthritis."

"Yes. That. Lucky if years. Likely for life. The doctors plan on talking to the Commander about banishing the sergeant."

"What?" Knobs exclaimed.

"I think she means permanent disability—early retirement."

"Yes, is that not the same thing?"

"For Pierowski, yeah. Yeah, it probably is."

One more tragedy Van Helsing would pay for.

After bringing us up to date on Clawfoot, Ertzbeth brought Jean up to speed on his illustrious ancestor's less famous undercover work. Jean insisted he'd never heard the Torre Annunziata story before, and knew absolutely nothing about the Varney fortune. Personally, I had no reason not to believe him. Unfortunately, ignorance wouldn't make him any less a target.

Lots of questions. I made a list.

One: We'd cleared up the mystery of the missing scars. Our real suspect was not Maarten, but Martin Van Helsing.

Two: Why had he visited my house? Clearly he wanted to complete his contract. But not finding me at home, it probably seemed foolish to tip his hand by harming Tami.

Three: Why kill Peggy? Because he's a heartless dick.

Four: Why steal the camera? See question three. It sounds like a smart-ass answer, even to me. But something told me Martin's inexorable douchebaggery might be the most important bit of data we had.

Five: Where the hell was he? Not a clue. B's people had spent four years tracking every single move of the wrong guy.

Six: Where were we compared to a week ago? Three steps behind Square One. Not only didn't we know where to find our killer, but our killer now knew we were after him, he had even greater incentive to kill all of us, and we'd managed to piss off his identical kung-fu cousin. Plus, we were two cops down. No joy in Mudville. Mighty Angus was striking out.

"Jean, how does one get in touch with the Van Helsing family? To hire them, I mean."

"I understand that in the early days one would have an announcement read at church services. Word would reach the Family through secret channels. Later, prospective clients placed personal advertisements in the newspaper. Up until a few years ago, when the Family was driven completely underground, one could post notices on electronic bulletin boards. In each case, the family would then contact the client. The family always controls the contact."

"So you've got no idea where the family is based, or how to get in touch with them on our terms?" asked Knobs.

"Amsterdam. New York. Paris. Calcutta."

"Those are big fucking cities."

"Oui. Fortunately, the Internet has made the world a much smaller place. Now it is nearly impossible to communicate without leaving some kind of trail. If either Van Helsing is still monitoring his usual networks, then we should be able to reach him. When either man responds, we shall track him!"

I called Lord B to find out how had first contacted Martin four years earlier. He provided us with a long list of "Van Helsing-approved" English-language newspapers, magazines and Websites. Some had gone out of business, but each one that remained still accepted classified ads. We were fairly certain anything we posted to them would be seen by Martin personally or forwarded to him by whatever passed for his Admin.

Contacting Maarten would require a little more guesswork. Having walked away from the family business he was, presumably, cut off from his European network. He'd probably suspect any inquiries appearing in tried-and-true Van Helsing conduits as traps. I know I would. But the Web provided a list of Dutch-language newspapers, magazines and online communities. It was worth a shot.

Each Van Helsing received a different message.

In Martin's publications, we planted a pro-forma personal ad with all the recommended Van Helsing red flags: looking for a guy with a big gun not afraid of the dark blah blah blah. The clincher, or so we were told, was to drop the name Mammon. The recommended Van Helsing-monitored Web sites turned out to be mostly gay dating services with names like Manhunt, joeblow and themineshaft. Not judging. If you're trying to camouflage ads with cheesy phrases like "man seeking man," "big gun," and "not afraid" you won't find a cozier home than Manhunt. We had some fun filling out the little online forms. They all asked for basically the same info:

Headline: Searching for my Fearless V.H.

About me: Man seeking Man

Location: New York, NY

Age: Timeless

Pets: Big dog that bites

Occupation: Contractor

Income: Unlimited

Religion (Optional): Mammon

Languages: English, Dutch

Interests: Hunting, the 2nd Amendment, Nightlife.

If that didn't get his attention, we'd have to send a flare up over Manhattan.

Maarten got a slightly different treatment. This is a rough translation from the Dutch: Man seeking man to come in out of the cold. Mammon is dead. Let's watch the sun set together.

THE OVERNIGHT: BLOOD FOR THE MARKED MAN

Jean set up a dummy e-mail account for each ad. We placed the ads and waited. To keep them from being traced back to us, he registered Martin's with an authentic anti-nightwalker group. He just never told them about it. We downloaded the responses using a laptop computer that we bought with the same group's credit card. We figured if Martin was good enough to hack the voice system at World Wide Plaza, he was good enough to run a "who is" search on the Web. In fact, we hoped he would.

We registered another e-mail address for the ads we placed in the Dutch publications and Web sites. This one could be traced back to Covenant House, the NYC-based shelter organization for young runaways. I hoped the symbolism might appeal to Maarten.

•••••

We got our first hit the very next morning. The dude was hungry for work. An e-mail from FearlessVH@vmail.com read:

"Loved your profile. I'm the Fearless V.H. you seek. I'm very good with big dogs. I think we can do a lot for each other, Mammon willing. How to win my affection? I'm a softy for gifts. Leave a token of your affection for me at the Madison Square Park Shake Shack. Ask for Seth. Leave the package for Twig. We'll see how things go from there."

"Great. He's got a sense of humor," said Knobs. "Last thing I ever want to deal with is a multiple murderer with a sense of humor."

"The Shake Shack. What is that?" I asked.

I was surprised when Ertzbeth answered. "It is a hamburger stand in the middle of the park. Very 1950s. Classic architecture and fabulous bacon cheese burgers. Or so my Peggy always said."

A drop off in public. Mixed blessing. Martin, or "Twig," would be somewhere nearby. We needed to find somebody who could deliver the package without tipping off Martin that the BNA was involved. Knobs had a great idea.

17

"I knew we were still buddies, Knobs!" Jay "The Voice" Kaminski struggled to open the gift-wrapped box, his right wrist in a styrene brace and his whole left arm in a cast and sling. He started to stutter. "Oh. Oh. Oh mygod." Inside was a Yankees cap with the signatures of the entire starting lineup of the 2000 World Series. "They swept, you know. They swept!"

"Yeah, I know," said Knobs.

Jay pulled the hat out, yanked off the nacho-cheese-stained cap he was still wearing and put the new one on his head. "Holy shit, Knobs! You are an amazing friend. Screw yuz all, your money's no good. I'm buying this round!"

"Listen Jay, I felt bad about wrecking your old cap, and, well, a little bit about wrecking your arms, so this was the least I could do. But I got stuck waiting for it and soon I'm gonna have to take an important conference call." Knobs vaguely waved his cell phone.

"Conference call?"

"Cop stuff. They're gonna call me here."

"On your cell phone? But can't ya…"

"Cop stuff."

"Oh. Yeah. I hear ya."

"So ya think you could you do me one little favor? I've got this package I need dropped off in the City..."

We stayed in the bar for about half an hour. Had to make it look good, right? When we got back to the car, Jean and Ertzbeth were waiting. "He will do it?" asked 'Beth.

"He's all over it," I said. "He would have driven to Quebec if Knobs asked him to. That's some gift. Where did you get a signed World Series Yankees cap?"

"Charged it to that anti-Nocturnals group. Didn't think B would mind."

Jay left right away. Knobs stayed at the Bastard to wait for him. The rest of us went back to my house to wait.

Driving his Harley with two broken arms, it took Jay about four and a half hours to get through the tunnel, down to 23rd street, drop off the package, turn around and get home. The package he delivered contained $10,000 in unmarked bills, courtesy of Lord B. We didn't send anybody to tail Jay because we didn't know how good Van Helsing was at counter-espionage. Besides, it would be completely out of character for Martin Van Helsing to harm a bag man. He was all about the cash flow. As we expected, Jay simply made the drop and came back, with no exciting stories to tell. Knobs pumped him for everything he saw and heard anyway, which was pretty much nothing. Seth turned out to be a kid in his mid-twenties who made a few extra bucks holding onto packages for his regular customers. Nobody suspicious on the street. Nobody followed Jay in or out. Everything went exactly as planned.

Knobs had been back at the house for no more than 20 minutes when Jean got a hit on the Dutch/English Maarten ads. We gathered around Jean's little cyber-nest in the living room. "Angus, it's from incredibleVH@yahoo.net. It says 'It's cold out here. Need to come in. Mammon can rot in hell.'"

"Can you trace the IP address or something, maybe see where it's coming from?"

"C'est impossible. Virtually. Unless the user possesses a static IP, like one would need for hosting one's own domain, IP addresses, they are dynamically generated by the ISP and, of course, no one has real-time access to the location of an individual…"

"I really don't need the IT class, Jean. What can you do for us?"

"I was just killing time." His laptop chimed like a meat timer. "The e-mail was typed on a Dell Dimension XPS, bought in Paramus, New Jersey with a Mastercard ending in the number 1784 and expiring… ooo next month. Let me get the rest of that credit card number, and we should have the owner of the computer!"

"Let me save you some time." I pulled out my wallet and fanned through my vast array of two credit cards. "Thought so. That's my computer. How's he doing that?"

"Well, he is either running some kind of remote desktop access software, like Timbuktu or a VNC variant, or he is in your office."

"Son of a bitch!"

I ran down the hallway, drawing my Glock as I ran, and hurtled through the doorway into my office. There I found Maarten Van Helsing sitting at my desk, drinking my scotch, looking at a Dutch porn site. "Sometimes I miss home so much," he said.

"Yeah. I don't blame you. What the hell are you doing here?"

"You invited me in."

"We invited you to 'come in from the cold.' It's an old cold-war spy thing. I didn't literally invite you into my house!"

"My mistake. Should I leave?"

"No! Stay right here. Ertzbeth! Jean!" As I turned toward the door, Ertzbeth pushed me aside and threw Maarten up against the wall. Before I could blink, she grabbed a rapier from a wall display and readied the point on Van Helsing's trachea.

"Ask me about Varney."

"Excuse me?"

"Ask me about Varney's Fortune. Now. Or I will pin you to the wall."

A tiny trickle of blood was already staining the neck of his t-shirt. Van Helsing remained calm. What's one more scar? "Ask me!"

"Where is Varney's Fortune?"

"Ask me who helped me throw Francis Varney into the volcano." 'Beth closed her eyes.

"Who helped you throw Francis Varney into the volcano?"

She opened her eyes. Handed me the sword. "This is not the man who murdered Peggy." Then she walked out of the room.

"What did I just survive?" Van Helsing asked, absently wiping the blood from his throat. "Was that who I thought it was?"

"The Blood Countess."

"Oh, my God. I hope I made a good impression."

"You didn't pee yourself, if that's what you're worried about. C'mon. We're all set up in the living room."

The living room was getting crowded. 'Beth, Jean, Maarten and I pulled up folding chairs and gathered around the coffee table, where Jean had set up his little cyber-nest: laptop, printer, high-speed satellite link, scanner and encryption router. Tami and Shelly stood in the kitchen doorway, a little star-struck over Maarten. Maarten, for his part, couldn't pry his eyes off Ertzbeth.

Knobs burst in with news of Jay's mission accomplished, and stopped dead when he saw Maarten. Without another word, he made a beeline for the kitchen doorway and placed himself between Maarten and Shelly. If he'd been a German Shepherd we would have been growling. Shelly peeked around his right triceps and said, "Baby, it's OK. We invited him, remember?"

Knobs waved his cellphone. "Suddenly our phones don't work anymore? Lotta civilians here, Angus." He wrapped his arm around Shelly, effectively blanketing her in muscle.

"Sorry Knobs. He's been here… well, I don't know how long he's actually been here… but we've been aware he was here for about five minutes."

Shelly pried Knobs' arm off her shoulder. "I am not a civilian."

He glanced briefly at her belly. "I wasn't talking about you."

Maarten broke the long awkward silence with more awkwardness. "You're the guy who wanted to fight me last week, aren't you?"

"Do we need to talk about this now?" asked Shelly. Knobs didn't say anything.

"You were like a crazy man! Tell me, Knobs, is it? Why you think you can beat me."

"Hello?" Shelly stepped between the two men. "You two are not fighting. Ever. So no point in even discussing it."

Van Helsing stood up and talked directly over the top of her blond head. "You seemed pretty convinced. Why?"

"Because I can."

"What makes you think that?"

"I don't think it. I know it."

Shelly waved her arms. "Jesus Christ! Family man in progress here! Not fighting the vampire killer!"

Van Helsing pursued it. "Tell me how."

"Nope." He looked to Shelly for approval. She gave it.

Van Helsing grinned. "Aren't we allies now? What harm can it do?"

Knobs wrapped both arms around Shelly again. "A week ago I thought you were a killer. Who knows what I'll think of you next week?"

"Very good! You know, I'm almost worried. For my cousin Martin, of course. I know you would not hurt a new friend. Right, new friend?"

Maarten put out his hand. Knobs reached out his own. Their eyes were locked. As their hands touched, Tami said, "You two start anything in my living room I'll kill you both. Got me?"

The two men laughed and shook hands. Almost like normal human beings.

"Let me tell you about our family," said Maarten, "so you know what you are up against. Friedrich Nietzsche wrote: 'Battle not with monsters lest ye become a monster, and if you gaze into the abyss, the abyss gazes also into you.' He might have written that as a personal note to my family. Erlicht Van Helsing was the first of the Van Helsing monster-hunters, in the early years of the 17th century. Having discovered the truth of the supernatural predators, and discovering within himself the courage and skill to defeat them, he was faced with a dilemma similar to yours, Angus. I wish he had chosen as wisely. You shared the truth with the world. Erlicht conspired to cover it up. Was he afraid of the Church? Afraid of ridicule? Or simply reluctant to live in poverty? Our family history doesn't say. All we know is that in 1632, Erlicht Van Helsing and his sons rode out across Europe to do battle with those who walked the night. By 1662, the Van Helsing name ranked among the wealthiest in the Netherlands. They lost it all when the South Sea Bubble crashed in 1711, but steadily regained it over the next hundred years. To this day, the Van Helsing family tree is pruned closer than any bonsai. Each male child is trained in martial arts and sciences from the day he can walk. Only the fittest, mentally and physically, are permitted to carry on the family name."

"You need permission to marry?" Asked Shelly.

"No. To reproduce. Certain mild drugs are quietly introduced into the culled cousins' diets. No one's harmed. No one's the wiser. Those who don't measure up as enforcers or management are simply never introduced to the real family business. Later they invariably find that their wives or husbands (always blame it on the in-laws) are tragically infertile. They are then offered management positions with one of our many small real estate or manufacturing companies. Offers which they are free to reject. They are, after all, just clippings. And life goes on.

"But those of us who do measure up—we receive training in skills that have been honed and passed down for a dozen generations. We are, without a doubt, the finest hunters of night-walkers on the planet." He looked Ertzbeth in the eye, trying to draw out some kind of understanding. It didn't work. "And each generation, we get better."

"But there is an even darker side to this, is there not?" asked Ertzbeth.

"You know this part as well as I do, Milady Bathory. Please. The floor is yours."

"I have battled the Van Helsing family many times over many years. Not, as you might think, because they hunt my kind. As you all now know, I have also hunted my own kind. No, I have harried the Van Helsings across the Carpathians, through France and right back to Amsterdam because of what they have done to the innocent villagers they purport to defend. When a terrified village burgher or priest called upon the Van Helsings, he would often promise the moon and stars just to have his village free of whatever scourge plagued it. The Van Helsing policy was iron-clad. A contract was a contract. If the village could not come up with payment the Van Helsings would pillage until they considered their debt paid. And the Van Helsings never forgive a debt. They were never paid for the Varney mission, in fact. And never will be. Be careful, Monsieur Vidocq. You have a deadly creditor at your elbow."

"Vidocq? Your ancestor was part of the Varney adventure?" Maarten smirked, his scars crinkling. "Fascinating."

Vidocq tried to look nonchalant. No dice. After a few awkward seconds he got up and moved his laptop to the dining room table.

"I am no longer a Van Helsing as you know us, Milady," Maarten protested. "Our mission has been banned. My family has disowned me for not pursuing you and Lord Ruthven. And they say I'm a disgrace for performing like a trained monkey for tips. As far as my family is concerned, I am a traitor to all they believe. This may be hard to believe, but I can be killed on sight. Now, I do not expect anyone here to trust me. I don't trust you. But please accept the fact that my family does not trust me either. You may as well use me in whatever capacity I can help, because I have nowhere else to go. Nothing else to do. I may not be able to be your friend, but I can be an excellent weapon."

I looked around the room. Tami, Shelly, Knobs and I weren't alone, as we'd been the night before the Armistice. We now had plenty of allies. Maarten Van Helsing. Jean Vidocq. Ertzbeth Bathory. Victor "Lord B" Ruthven. All we needed was a plan.

· · · · ·

We heard from Martin again Thursday afternoon: Via e-mail: "Your gift was very generous. I'm sure I'll find that you have ten times that much affection when I finally meet your dog. L.O.L. I do hope you're not in a hurry, though, because I have some business to take care of and I'm afraid your dog will have to wait a few days.

Love, F.V.H."

I didn't like the sound of "business to take care of." Neither did Maarten or Ertzbeth.

"Van Helsings are ALL business," said Maarten. "If he's delaying a $100,000 payday for killing a simple werewolf— no offense Shelly— then he has got something huge in the works."

"Marlton, it need not be something new at all," Ertzbeth said. "Our enemy now has six unfulfilled contracts. The Varney treasure, Angus, Knobs, Tami, Shelly and now our imaginary werewolf. Each payable upon receipt of a corpse. The more obligations he has, the more options he has. The more options..."

"The less predictable he becomes," I finished. "Yes. I know. But we have to flush him out. And I'm not hearing any better ideas."

Before we broke for dinner, Maarten nudged Knobs. "C'mon. Tell me."

"Nope."

• • • • •

We sat and stewed for three more days. Lord B, who was stewing all alone in Washington, was burning up the phone lines with us, as well as every intelligence agency he could strong-arm into helping us. Jean was hacking every network I-24/7 could plug him into. Maarten tried tapping into whatever contacts he had left, but found them sorely depleted since his family declared him a burned asset. Knobs, Shelly, Tami and I put on a show of normalcy. We went running every day as usual, with radios velcroed into our shorts and Bluetooth microphone buds shoved into our ears. Even knowing that help was seconds away, we felt like we were wearing bulls-eyes on our backs. I'd never been so glad to get back into my own house before.

When the tension finally broke, it broke all at once.

The sun was on the rise.

I was watching the news.

Jean was scanning briefs on I-24/7 and Tami was on the phone explaining to Cathy, her boss at the hospital, why she couldn't come into work again.

As the anchor desk cut away for breaking news from Washington, Jean yipped that we had another e-mail from Martin.

"Cathy, what's wrong?" Tami asked.

"He wants a meeting!" Jean cried.

"We now take you to Washington, D.C. where Biff Sloane is reporting live from The Castle on the Mall."

"Cathy! Is the sergeant alright? Cathy pick up!"

"Aujourd'hui! He insists on meeting today!"

"Firefighters are struggling frantically to contain the blaze which mysteriously engulfed The Castle just a few minutes ago. Home to the Bureau of Nocturnal Affairs, the 150 year old structure is mostly stone."

"Angus! It's Sergeant Pierowski. He's on a rampage at the hospital!"

"Monsieur Wellstone. This is our opportunity. Shall I gather everyone?"

"…and that's why the fire has them baffled. Hold on—I'm getting a report that Director Carter is at a luncheon with Habitat for Humanity in Georgetown. That's good news. No word yet on Director Ruthven."

I didn't know which way to turn. "Tami. Hang up and call 911. Tell them Angus said to send McInnes, Olanski and a tranquilizer gun. Knobs and I'll go over, too. Vidocq, stall him! Get Maarten and Ertzbeth on it. Set something up, but make it smart and keep it safe. Baby, please keep an eye on this news report. It's Lord B's office. He's probably sleeping off an absinthe binge as the building burns around him! Goddamnit where's Knobs?"

"He took Shelly home. Just to shower and grab a change of clothes. They've got an important prenatal today."

"Timing. Timing sucks."

I grabbed my cell phone. "Call Knobs." It autodialed as I ran for the car.

Both Knobs and Shelly were waiting for me when I got to their doorstep. "Shel, this is dangerous," I began.

"Don't even start. What are you gonna do against a nine foot Kodiak bear? At least I'm a werewolf, ferchristsake."

"Yeah, a werewolf carrying a baby…"

Knobs cut me off, his face a stone slab. "Angus, give it over. Think I didn't just lose this argument? Take her with us, she's in the middle of the shit with us. Active words: with us. We leave her here and we're leaving her alone, unprotected. And she'd just follow us anyway."

Shelly was right. In danger with us or in danger alone. There were no safe options.

We got to the hospital in under five minutes. Just in time to see a Godzilla-run of doctors and patients come streaming out the door marked Emergency Entrance. Knobs tried one last time: "Honey, please. This is gonna be hell. You get hurt again I'll never forgive myself."

That got her. She stayed in the car. And Knobs has never forgiven himself.

We sprinted through the halls to the ICU. Even if we hadn't known the way, we could have followed the sound of screaming and breaking glass. Waving our badges, we pushed past the hospital security staff, some of whom struggled to move patients to safety while others maintained an ad hoc rear guard against whatever waited beyond two blue automatic sliding doors.

For the sake of our long friendship, we went in empty-handed. As soon as the doors slid back, roaring screams buffeted us like a high wind. At the far end of the corridor, Clawfoot convulsed in agony, tearing the hospital down around him. A gigantic IV still swung from his right arm, flopping around as he flailed. Blood and spit pooled and spattered at the corners of his jaw. He roared. Lashed out. Smashed, clawed, bit and stomped. The floors, walls and even the ceiling were shredded. I feared for the structural integrity of the wing. Clawfoot saw us. No recognition. Just rage. With one staggering step he moved six feet closer to us. I looked at Knobs. He nodded. We had no choice. We drew our Colt revolvers, dumped the normal rounds into our hands and clicked in speedloaders fitted with silver tipped rounds.

Just as we locked the barrels home, I heard Jimmy McInnes yell "Don't shoot!"

Maggie Olanski scrambled around the corner with the department's single-shot tranquilizer air rifle. She threw it to me. I quickly checked the dosage. There was enough in each dart to drop a werewolf, but that wouldn't be enough to take down all 500 pounds of Clawfoot.

I'd have to hit him twice. Shoot. Reload. Shoot again.

Sounded like a plan. What wound up happening was more like shoot, run like hell, drop two darts 'cause I'm still running like hell, reload, and finally turn and fire the second dart point blank into Clawfoot's sweeping paw. The second dart dropped him.

The first doctor to stick his head back into the corridor got a pass; I let him check on Pierowski. The second one I grabbed by the tie. "What happened here? That man's been sedated for almost a week because of pain. Who the hell woke him up?"

"I have no idea, detective!" The doc was shaking, probably going into shock himself. "Look! He's still wearing the IV. He is sedated!"

Knobs grabbed the huge bag of fluid dangling from Pierowski's fur-covered limb. He read the label. "This isn't a sedative. This is aconite!"

"Wolfsbane?" asked the doctor. "You can't give Wolfsbane to a full lycanthrope! The pain could kill them!"

"I know that!" said Knobs, ripping the needle from Pierowski's arm and throwing the bag at the doctor. "I didn't give it to him. One of you did. And when I find out who's responsible for this I'll make this mess look like Sunday school."

"Knobs. Calm down."

"No! Somebody here almost killed Clawfoot. Almost made US kill Clawfoot!" He waved the pistol he'd recently loaded with silver. "I am sick of everybody I care about being a target. Goddamnit why can't they fucking pick on some other goddamned town? I swear to fucking Marduk I wish we'd just killed Gustaffson that night and buried his hairy ass under the end zone at Giants Stadium." He threw the aconite bag at the wall. It burst, splashing into a pool of Clawfoot's blood, where it sizzled like bacon.

I put my arm around Knobs' shoulder and walked him out of the hospital.

"I swear to God, Angus. I'm not sure how much more I can take."

Behind us, Maggie Olanski knelt down next to Clawfoot, holding his paw and telling him, over and over, he'd be OK.

He'd been told that a lot over the last week. And, well, he wasn't OK.

The worst was yet to come. We got to the car and found a note under the windshield. Knobs went around to the passenger side as I pulled the note off the window. "Thanks for the token of your affection. I went ahead and took care of your dog problem. Love, F.V.H.

"P.S. KaChing!"

"NO! NO! Please GOD NO!" Knobs grabbed and tugged at the locked door. I groped in my pocket for the electric key. Knobs smashed the window with his gunbutt as I popped the lock open. He reached in and pulled Shelly's limp form from the back seat. A small trickle of blood ran down her face from a bullet hole in the center of her forehead.

They got her on the operating table in minutes. David Applebaum, the Israeli doctor who had saved her life a year earlier, burst through the crash doors trailing a team of trauma specialists. He reached the table and stopped. He studied the two wounds—the entrance and the much larger exit—for less than two seconds before putting his hands up in defeat. "She's gone."

He reached for a sheet to pull over her head as he checked his watch to declare time of death. Knobs grabbed his wrist. "Do something."

"There is nothing to do. There's too much trauma to the brain."

"You brought her back last time!" Last time, she'd had her throat ripped out by Lars Gustaffson. Applebaum had treated the wound with a Golem patch. Shelly'd been turned into a werewolf, but she'd survived. "You brought her back!"

"Yes, I did. And I could do something even more drastic this time, but you wouldn't want that to happen to her. Her brain is dead.

Let her body rest in peace."

The door behind me opened and Tami rushed in. She saw Shelly's body, seeping blood from the exit wound at the back of her skull, and buckled. "Oh Goddess. Not again." I caught her. She recovered, squeezed my hand and reached for Knobs. He didn't respond but she hugged him and held on tight anyway.

Knobs needed time alone, but I didn't want him armed. He was on the verge of a very dangerous breakdown. As I gently took his weapons, he nodded. He thought it was a good idea, too.

I took Tami's hand and we left the room as quietly as we could. The doctors and nurses followed. I squeezed Applebaum's slumped shoulder as he passed. There was nothing ethical he could have done. Since scientists have started studying vampires and lycanthropes, they've discovered lots of ways to bring back the dead. But almost all of them reek of the Monkey's Paw. We couldn't do that to poor Shelly.

We took Tami's car. Mine was now a crime scene. "We've got to go to the station. I need to talk to Todd and we've got to find Lord B."

"That's what I was coming to tell you. They found Lord B. He was in his office."

"They found his body?"

"No! He escaped! I saw the whole thing on the news. There was this series of loud explosions, and the security bars outside B's office just flew out across the Mall."

"Finally got to use the shotgun."

"Smoke poured out of the window. The next thing you know, this black shadow climbs out and goes straight up the brick wall! You could barely make him out because of all the smoke. He ran across the roof and dove off into a grove of trees in the garden out back. He's singed but safe."

"It's broad daylight. That must have been some smoke cover."

"It looked almost theatrical. The smoke was very thick. It gave him plenty of cover from the sunlight. And the trees did the rest. The firemen got him under a tarp as soon as he hit the ground."

"It was another trap."

"Another trap?"

"This whole thing. Spiking Clawfoot's IV. It was a trap just to get us out of the house. To separate us. Setting the fire at the Castle. Just another trap to smoke Lord B out. Literally smoke him out. This Martin is very smart. A lot smarter than we are. If we don't get smarter fast, we're all gonna wind up…"

"Like Shelly."

"And her baby. Yeah. Let's get to the station."

I could have called Todd, but I didn't trust our phones. Martin had seen right through our phony personal ads, which we'd half-expected, but somehow he also knew where we were all the time. That I hadn't anticipated. But why not? This guy had rigged the comms at a high-security New York skyscraper. Of course he could trace our phones. I should have thought of that earlier, but I didn't, because I was too busy being the clever superhero. I'd tried to draw him out and instead I'd drawn him a map of our entire plan. I'd been cocky and reckless. Somewhere along the way I'd let the celebrity high of being the Twilight Cop go to my head, and now Shelly and Knobs were paying for it. The truth is, I'm still not equipped for this stuff. I'm trained to handle suburban bad guys. And it was becoming brutally clear that this Van Helsing asshole was simply out of my league.

The station was nearly deserted when we got there. Martin Van Helsing had really done a job on our roll call. Pierowski and Franco, both disabled. Pierowski most likely permanently. Knobs, still at the hospital with Shelly. Olanski and McInnes, guarding Pierowski. Knobs and I had been assigned to the Van Helsing case, which had pulled me away from the station for two weeks already. This case had effectively put six of us on the DL for the foreseeable future. We only have a force of 16 total. No wonder Todd was so pissed at Lord B.

"Wellstone, before you even start: no, you cannot pull any more men and no, you cannot 'borrow' some armor and ammunition." Todd's shoulders almost filled the narrow corridor between the briefing room and the holding cells. Her feet planted firmly and her hands in fists on her hips, she reminded me of Little John. I wouldn't have been surprised to hear her say, "You shall not pass!" I know she was thinking it.

"Commander, I'm not looking to put more cops in the crosshairs. Believe me, I didn't expect to bring this war home with me. It's the last thing I wanted. But let's talk somewhere else." I gestured around, trying to mime 'bugs.' That's not as easy as it sounds. I finally pulled out my notebook and wrote 'Station may be bugged. Talk outside.' She looked at me like I'd just sprouted a garden gnome on my shoulder, but she followed me to the cops-only lot out back. Tami came with us. There was no way I was leaving her alone until I had Martin on a slab. Maybe not ever.

And in case you didn't catch my conditions just now, let me make it crystal clear: Yes, I had made up my mind that this guy was ending his career on a slab. He'd done too much damage to live. Peggy, Ertzbeth, Clawfoot and now Shelly? He had to go. Plus, he held an unbreakable contract to kill both Tami and me. Lord B had put me in a real bind. New Jersey doesn't have a death penalty and New York doesn't use the one it has. So this one was going to be on me. I'm no vigilante. I'll put my own life on the thin blue line any day. But there wasn't a chance in hell I would condemn my wife to forty years of terror, just waiting for this psychopath to escape from some corporate felon factory and track us down again.

In retrospect, I probably shouldn't have said all of that out loud in front of Commander Todd. But as she, Tami and I stood in the parking lot in the fading light of the July afternoon, I found myself explaining exactly how I intended to put a permanent end to the man who'd crippled Clawfoot Pierowski and murdered Dr. Shelly Johnson. Todd didn't flinch. We talked about what we needed to do to end this. And she told me what it would cost me if I lost another of her men or women.

"Angus, you didn't bring this war home," Todd began. "Victor Ruthven did. Don't even start with me. I know he's your friend, and believe me, as a 60-year old black woman from Newark, New Jersey, I can tell you there is not a person on God's green earth who more appreciates your unshakable respect for diversity. You've told me it's what people do, not what they are, that matters. Now, you were talking about vampires and werewolves at the time, but you were also talking about me. Shut up. You didn't know you were but you were. It's not always what you say, it's what people hear. Now you have to accept that your rules work both ways. Ruthven isn't a problem because he's a vampire. He's a problem because he lied to you. Used you. Put your family in jeopardy and got two young women killed. You choose to trust him, you go right ahead and I'll go along because I trust you. But if this goes balls up, you're done. You understand me?"

I wasn't sure I did. I looked to Tami for support, but her face was a blank. Shoulders back, head up, but not arguing with a word Todd was saying.

"Done, Angus," Todd clarified. "Retired. Whatever pension you've accrued, you'll get. Whatever you can get for the house, take it. Because one more Hawthorne cop gets hurt, or God forbid killed, and you will be persona non grata in Passaic County. You pull this off, be a hero…"

"I don't…"

"Of course you don't. If you did, we wouldn't be having this conversation at all. But you're a magnet for this shit, Angus. I need to see you can put down what you call up. If you can't, I have to make sure you take your shit to someone else's town. And Heaven help whoever lets you in."

"'Lets me in'?" I echoed. "You make me sound like a vampire."

Tami finally spoke, her voice small, just a little bit broken, "Birds of a feather, Angus."

My job. My house. My town. Did Todd think she was raising the stakes? Martin Van Helsing was out to kill Tami. Knobs. Me. I was about to tell Todd she could shove her threats when she beat me to it.

"I know none of that matters, Angus. You've got murders to prevent. I'm just being honest with you. I figure after the way your boyfriend has been treating you, you might appreciate it. Now let's get back to your plan. Hand me that list."

We went back inside. As Todd and I worked, Tami banged on a cell door with a nightstick to screw with any sound surveillance. First the Commander opened up the evidence room. She pulled out a half-dozen fancy little pre-paid cell phones that had been confiscated from low-level high school coke dealers. "Charge 'em up, don't give anyone else the numbers and you two are effectively off the grid." That took care of our phone tap problem. "And you have my permission to bring in that covert ops team you've been saddled with. They can base here temporarily, but I want an assurance from Mr. Ruthven that one, they answer to me, and two, any fuck-ups are his responsibility."

"Sounds fair." I stepped outside again and made two calls from the new phones. The first was to check on B and get him in the loop. Before I could cut off, Todd grabbed the phone and extracted even more assurance than she'd gotten from me. I only heard one side of the call, but I wouldn't be surprised if B agreed to emigrate to Transylvania if anything went wrong.

The next call was to Maarten and Jean at my house. Jean answered.

"Don't say anything, my home phone might be compromised. Put Maarten on for a second."

"Maarten, he is not here."

"Where the hell is he?"

"Je ne sais pas! He left right after you did."

"Is Ertzbeth?"

"Still asleep."

"Good. Go check on her and when you're done, I want you to take that bag of tricks you've got and sweep every wire in my house. You set up to do that?"

"Oui. But have we not just told Martin we know of the bugs?"

I glanced across the street and saw a black Mercedes roadster with rolled-up tinted windows. The driver's side window glided open to reveal a small parabolic listening antenna. Martin grinned and roared off down the road. "He knows." In the shadows of the car I thought I saw other heads, as well. "Double-check every door. No! Wake Ertzbeth up first. Check every window and arm yourself. Over and under is in the hall closet. I'll be there in five minutes!"

Tami's poor little Saturn station wagon couldn't keep up with a Mercedes Roadster if they were both falling off a cliff, so Martin beat me home by nearly two minutes. Tami was with me. That had been the toughest split-second call I'd ever had to make. I knew I was rolling into another trap. Should I leave her at the station, or was that the real trap? Did Van Helsing want to split us up, and get us one at a time? Should I bring her with me, and risk making her an easy target, right in the crossfire? Finally she grabbed my hand and made the decision for me. "I won't let anything happen to you," she said, and ran for the car.

We pulled around the corner to find four men on the front lawn. I handed Tami my Glock 21C. Safety's in the trigger so there are no switches to worry about. Compensated to reduce recoil and best of all, 13 rounds in the clip. One look at our opposition and I handed her another full clip. I grabbed my backup Sig Sauer 9mm off my boot. 7 rounds in the clip. One in the chamber. If I couldn't drop four guys with eight shots, I'd be dead anyway.

I fully intended to get out of the car and start shooting. But 25 years of proper police work refused to stand down. I yelled "Freeze!" As if they hadn't seen me pull up. Surprisingly, they did freeze for a moment. Long enough for me to size them up. And, of course, for them to size me up. There was Martin, long and lean just like his cousin, but a few years younger and a lot less weathered. With him were three other guys I'd never seen before. One was almost as tall as Martin, but not as thin. Blond hair with one of those ugly chin-only Amish/hipster beards. The other two were both clearly Eastern European. Just under six feet tall, both with thick brown hair and bushy eyebrows, something about them screamed "gypsy." All four were wiry as all hell. They wore loose-fitting linen suits with, of course, lots of pockets. And all four had the tell-tale bulges in their shirts that can really only mean body armor. Okey dokey. Head shots is it, then. None of them had a weapon in hand, but that didn't mean anything. I'd watched Maarten make knives appear out of nowhere like a magician doing card tricks.

And what do you know? No sooner had they taken my measure than bushy-brow #1 produced a shuriken. Faster than I could see, he sailed it across the yard and buried it in my thigh. Hurt like a... well, like a blade stuck in my thigh. I think the guy expected me to drop, because he turned and high-fived his brother. I shot the top of his head clean off. Dum-Dum bullets. I've been stabbed so many times in the last six years my body looks almost as bad as Maarten's. One little knife wound wasn't going to spoil my aim. Tami cheered, and fired two shots at Martin. So Martin started throwing knives at her. Let me tell you, those dent-resistant panels Saturn advertises? Worth every penny. The look on Martin's face when his first dagger bounced back at him was priceless. And it allowed me to get off another shot. Caught him too low—right in the chest. He staggered backward, but recovered immediately. That's when he threw all his focus at me and I knew I was dead. He pulled two steel balls, about the size of golfballs, from somewhere in the folds of his pants and threw them both. One after the other. The first hit my gun hand. I heard a crack. The second hit the gun, knocking it clean out of my freshly broken fingers.

He signaled his two remaining friends toward the front door of my house. Then he pulled a long dagger from one of those damned pockets and came at me. He moved like a mongoose. By the time my brain had kissed my feet goodbye, he was already across the yard and slicing at my throat. Then he stumbled, and tumbled right past me. I made some distance, fast. He bounced back up, face flushed with shock and rage. Clearly, this guy hadn't fallen down since he was in diapers. Even his two remaining buddies stopped and stared. He barked an order: "Keep going!" And they did.

He looked down and so did I. That's when I saw Xena, my favorite baton, glistening in the grass at his feet. I put a lot of faith in that silver-capped nightstick—a very precious gift from Tami —but I doubted she had attacked Martin on her own. "Hello, cousin!" called Maarten, stepping out from the middle of a large rhododendron. He was stripped to the waist and barefoot. He was also painted in camouflage greens and browns. He'd probably been sitting in that bush since I left for the hospital. He stepped over and addressed the fresh corpse. "And hello Cousin... Isaak, is it?"

"I've got him!" Martin yelled. "Get Vidocq!" All three men moved at the same time. Martin pulled a sai to complement the long knife and dropped into an offensive crouch. Blondie and bushy-brow

#2 sprang up the three low steps to my front door. As the tall one reached for the doorknob, the whole door flew off its hinges and carried them both backwards down the stairs. The telltale report of the over-and-under's double-barreled blast followed a fraction of a second later. Tami, both thugs and I were all staggered by the sound, but Martin and Maarten didn't even flinch. I shook it off and looked up to see Jean Vidocq reloading in my very open doorway. I took the opportunity to grab my fallen weapon with my left hand.

Martin lunged at his cousin, who evaded to the left. Another thrust, left, missed as well. Martin launched a complicated pattern of cuts and thrusts, each of which Maarten managed to avoid. He seemed to anticipate each attack. And that might even be true, since they had the same training. But Maarten was unarmed. And Martin had a practically endless supply of sharp surprises.

At the doorway, Vidocq finished chambering the round, stepped out and covered the two under the door. I stood almost hypnotized by the speed and ferocity of the fight between the two Van Helsings. "Shoot him."

I snapped out of it. Maarten ducked another swipe and tagged his cousin with a jab. His intricate footwork brought him within two yards of me. "Shoot him."

"What?"

"Shoot him. This is exhausting. What are you waiting for?"

"Oh. OK." Of course, that's easier said than done with a Van Helsing. And with my left hand. My target saw me raise my weapon and moved to put Maarten between us. I got three shots off. One hit him in the body armor. Another winged his left arm. Then Martin threw a roundhouse kick. Maarten ducked it easily, which was, apparently, exactly the idea, because I was standing right behind him. The kick nailed me right behind the ear. Everything went black for a fraction of a second. It couldn't have been longer than that because I was conscious again by the time my body hit the lawn. As I looked up, Maarten looked down to see if I was OK and Martin thrust, burying the long knife in his cousin's ribs. Suddenly we were both on the ground, my head spinning and Maarten's blood spraying my lawn like a garden hose. Martin pushed his advantage immediately, closing in with both blades, and got spun right onto his ass as Tami opened up with the .45 from the shelter of the passenger door. She caught him once in the thigh and twice in the torso, which gave him one bleeder and probably two cracked ribs. This was a .45, after all. Body armor or not, he wasn't getting up fast this time. Tami kept shooting, which drove Vidocq back into the house. The two he had been covering scrambled across the lawn toward the Mercedes. I heard the fateful 'click' of an empty clip. The shooting had stopped. Martin staggered to his feet, wincing and holding his ribs, and started to sprint toward our Saturn and Tami. I got a foot out and tripped him up. He recovered quickly, but not before I heard the reassuring 'chunk' of a fresh clip sliding home. He heard it, too. Change of plans. He ran for the Mercedes. His cousins didn't wait for him. They were already burning rubber as he grabbed the back door handle, yanked it open and pulled himself inside. I watched the thought cross her face, but Tami resisted the urge to get out and fire after the vehicle. There'd been enough gunplay in this suburban neighborhood for one day.

The sound of police sirens gave me permission to pass out.

18

A lot of people got a lot of work done while I dozed. First of all, I was surprised to wake up in a holding cell. The door was open, so I figured I wasn't under arrest, but it was still a shock. The cell next to me wasn't open. And it was full. Really full. Somebody had bolted three hospital gurneys together to make a bed fit for Clawfoot Pierowski in his full, incapacitated ursine glory. An intricate web of tubes and plastic pouches were duct-taped in and among the bars. The first thing I did was check the labels. I couldn't help myself. Thorazine. Perfect.

To my right, Maarten was unconscious in another makeshift hospital room. His ribs were taped, and he had over a dozen bandages over the rest of his body. I guess Martin had been scoring more points than I'd realized.

The next thing I noticed was that my leg was howling at me. From the hip to the ankle, it was absolutely on fire. I looked down. The right leg of my jeans had been cut off six inches above the knee. My thigh was bandaged. I fished under the cot and found my running shoes. Time to see what else the elves had been up to.

The corridors were empty. The briefing room, on the other hand, was full to capacity. Todd was having an intense tete a tete with

Lord B—in person (how long had I been out?). Vidocq had taken our communications server cabinet apart and was attaching little gray boxes to everything in sight. McInnes, Franco, with his jaw wired shut, and Olanski were cleaning and loading weapons. Tami sat listening intently to some story Ertzbeth was sharing. I kept walking. No one in there needed my help right away. I wanted to see if all my arrangements had been taken care of. I got my answer at the front lobby.

The lobby's the biggest open space in the station, after the briefing room. So it was where Knobs was putting four special operatives through a very special and very sweaty kata that he'd put together himself. He heard me come in. Without turning he said, "Angus, you should learn this."

"We don't have five years. Work out the Brothers Grim here—they know what you're talking about." All five were slowly executing an excruciatingly precise set of tiny movements. Their impressive muscles flexed and bulged. I greeted each of them, and they gave tight tiny nods in return. "Michaelo. Boulad. Reilly. Kestler, how's the hand?" The hand Maarten impaled was taped, splinted and bandaged.

"Hurts like a motherfucker sir."

"Good to hear it. Don't shoot at horses."

"No sir."

"Glad you could all make it. We're going to need your help. Van Helsing—your old instructor—brought reinforcements. Knobs, you OK?"

"Long as I keep moving. So why don't you go check on something else? We're kind of busy here."

"Yeah, about that. Busy doing what?"

"Training."

"These guys auto-pilot ready yet?" I asked, nodding toward the Brothers Grim.

"What? Oh, yeah. They can run the moves for a while." Knobs spoke to Mikaelo. "Run 'em through the 'Crushing Glacier' for a few minutes. I'll be right back."

Mikaelo wrapped her arms in an X across her chest and face. "You heard the man. Form up!"

The other three assumed the same position and fell in line next to their superior officer. Together, they rocked slowly, inching a huge desk across the floor with their thighs.

"I have no idea what the hell that is, Knobs. You sure you're on this?"

Knobs walked me a few yards down the corridor. "If I'm not, we're fucked, right?"

"Pretty much."

"Then I'm on it."

"OK, but if we survive, some day I'm gonna write about this, so you feel like telling me what the hell you're planning?"

"Boulders for diamonds."

"..."

"Vampires are diamonds," he said. "Hard, eternal. But they've got a handful of very specific vulnerabilities. You hit them in just the right place, like the heart, with just the right amount of force, they shatter."

"OK, that's vampire. We're not training for vampires."

"No, but the Van Helsings are!" Knobs face brightened with the first hint of a smile I'd seen since he'd left Shelly's body in the hospital. "It takes a very precise instrument to shatter a diamond. Or to fight a vampire. Now, what happens if you take a precision instrument like a jeweler's hammer to a granite boulder?"

"I have no idea."

"You break the fucking hammer, Angus!"

"But granite is softer than diamond."

"Exactly!"

"..."

"It's bigger, Angus, with so many soft, vulnerable spots they don't matter. You bang away with a jeweler's hammer and…"

"Wait a minute. It's like water and stone, Knobs! Sand and stone. You keep chipping with a little hammer, eventually the stone is gonna lose."

"In a hundred years. A thousand. And you'll go through a lot of hammers before that happens. Trust me, Angus. I saw it on the field at the Ren Faire. You saw it yourself when they brought knives to a gunfight. These guys are precision tools—best I've ever seen—but they're equipped to split diamonds. We're gonna be boulders. Now get outta here. Kinda busy."

"Gotcha."

I hobbled in to the briefing room. Tami started to make a fuss but I shushed her. "I'm fine, Angel," I whispered. I went and sat down with B and Todd. "Hey, Smoky Joe. How long have you been here?"

"I arrived only a half hour ago, by helicopter. You look terrible. Shouldn't you be sleeping?"

"How long have I slept already?"

"A little over six hours. You lost a lot of blood and took a bad blow to the head. Dr. Applebaum was here for a short while, and patched you all up. Your family physician, Dr..."

"Conlan."

"Right. The vampire doctor. She arrived after dusk to check on you and Sergeant Pierowski. They both think you might have a concussion, but we wouldn't let you out of our sights long enough to get x-rayed. Survive this, and I promise all the ice-packs you can use, at Uncle Sam's expense."

"Big spender," I said. I asked Todd: "How's Maarten? That knife in the ribs looked pretty terminal."

"He should recover. Believe it or not, Applebaum says the man's been through worse. Some of those bigger scars line up with major organs. That's one hard-to-kill boy in there."

"But he has got to stay put," added B. "He probably survived the other wounds by getting first-class care immediately. The Van Helsings can afford it. Now that he's been cut off, all we can offer for the time being is this makeshift M.A.S.H. unit of ours."

Tami crossed the room with a cup of coffee. "Thanks, Angel." I turned to Todd. "I'm glad you took my advice and set us up in here. This building is as close to a fortress as we've got. Soundproof, bullet proof. Mostly fireproof. Plus, all the gunfights at my place are driving down the property values. Let's keep this away from innocent bystanders."

"Agreed," said Todd. "As soon as Vidocq secures our phones and Internet, we'll be ready to take this fight back to Van Helsing. On our terms this time. Remember what we talked about."

I grunted affirmative. I got up and hobbled over to join Tami and Ertzbeth. They both greeted me with kisses, which made the pain in my leg go away for a few minutes. "Ertzbeth's been filling me in on some of the trivia surrounding the Varney case," said Tami.

"Really. Trivia, huh? I gotta tell you, 'Beth, the things you and B consider trivia scares me sometimes. Funny story: See, B thought the fact that he'd hired assassins to kill us all was trivia. With that in mind, is there any trivia you might like to share with me?"

"My dear brave Angus, I have held none of that sort of critical minutiae back. No, I have been sharing with Tami the rest of the volcano story. It can harm no one now. You know who all but one of the conspirators was. There was myself, Lord Byron, now called Victor "Lord B" Ruthven, Eugene Francois Vidocq, founder of the French Surete, and one other, whom I called Mr. Black."

"That's right! Whatever happened to Mr. Black? The last thing I heard he was holding the pass below Vesuvius against Abraham Van Helsing and his men."

"Mr. Black survived, as I knew he would. Abraham Van Helsing had five mercenaries under his command. Mercenaries, in general, enjoy shooting people, but are not very tolerant of being shot. Mr. Black only had to kill two of them before the rest abandoned the chase and went back their regiments. He rejoined us later in Paris."

"So I assume the name Mr. Black is like Mr. Jones or Mr. Smith. Who is Mr. Black?"

"Mr. Black was a man I saved from an angry mob one night in Scotland. Having escaped from more than my share of torch-wielding hordes myself, I sympathized with his plight. Perhaps you have heard of the infamous Burke and Hare? The Resurrection Men? They provided disinterred corpses for the anatomists of the 19th century to study. William Hare and his partner William Burke were infamous for providing the freshest corpses of all."

"I don't think I like where this is going," I said.

"Oh, yes, ever the detective, my brave warrior. Two Irishmen living in Scotland, Burke and Hare, gave up grave robbing for the much more lucrative and less back-breaking method of murder. They killed a half-dozen guests at Hare's boarding house, and sold the bodies to medical students. Brilliant, yes?"

"Well, since you had to rescue one of them from a mob, I'm going with Brilliant, no."

"Exactly! They were caught. Mr. Hare—whose original idea it was—testified against his partner, Mr. Burke, who was hanged for crimes he had never wanted to commit in the first place. Mr. Hare had to change his name and flee the country—in fact he had to flee numerous countries. He drank, you see, and often forgot that murder is not polite conversation in most public houses. And that is how I met him. Running from an angry mob in Brittany. I pulled him into my carriage. He introduced himself as Billy Black. I recognized him immediately from the tabloids in England and so I introduced myself as the Angel of Death, come to demand penance for all the suffering he had caused. He never questioned an order from that night forward."

"So you had a cold-blooded murderer in your employ?"

"Ah! But he was not a murderer while in my employ. Instead, he assisted me in many conflicts, heroically risking his life against countless monsters far worse than himself. I, the Blood Countess, turned a murderer into a force for justice!"

"How do you account for the moral turnaround?"

"I did nothing with his morals. Merely his actions. Inside, Mr. Black remained an unrepentant beast for all of his days. But he was so terrified of The Angel of Death that he never took another life—or even another drink—without my specific instructions. Ironically, Mr. Black was terrified that I would kill him, when, in fact, he saved me countless times. "

"So that accounts for the four people who knew about the Varney fortune. You, B, Vidocq and Black. I assume Black didn't have any family?"

"You assume wrong. He had children whom he had abandoned in Ireland many years earlier. I insisted he send letters and money back to them. And so he did. I know for certain that he told them all about the Vesuvius adventure. I have remained very close to his family through the many, many years. In fact, whenever possible, I have kept a family member in my employ."

"Shouldn't we get some protection for them?" I asked. "Where do they live? Are they still called Hare? Or Black?"

"No, Angus. Do not waste your energy. They are neither Hare nor Black. And they are far beyond our help now. Van Helsing has already destroyed the last of the descendants of Billy Black. Her name was Peggy O'Farrel."

"Peggy? Peggy was the fourth who knew where you hid the Varney treasure? Why didn't you tell us?"

"Like you said, it was trivia. She is gone and cannot be questioned. I am just grateful he did not do to her what he did to me."

"I'm sorry, 'Beth, but this is not trivial at all. Martin Van Helsing knew who the fourth conspirator was the whole time. What did you tell us about the Shake Shack?"

"Peggy recommended the Bacon Cheese Burgers."

"The arrogant bastard left us a clue and we walked right past it! He sent us to one of Peggy's favorite places. He'd been watching her!"

Tami jumped in. "That doesn't make any sense. If he knew who Peggy was, why not take her? Maybe he was just following her to get access to Ertzbeth."

"No. There's more to it than that. If he knew where Peggy ate lunch downtown, he had somebody on her all the time. There's no way he could have been caught by surprise at the apartment. I think he had planned on catching Peggy when she came home and playing the two of you off each other. Tell me, 'Beth. If you knew he was going to... well, if you thought he was going to..."

"To keep him from doing to Peggy what he had done to me, I would have given him anything. Any secret. Any treasure. My own existence I would have sacrificed."

Tami said, "And I believe Peggy would have done the same."

"I do as well," said Ertzbeth.

"So that was his real plan," I said. "He probably never expected to break you with torture. He intended to use Peggy against you—or you against Peggy. 'Beth, I don't think we ever asked you about a camera…"

"Daguerre's camera obscura?"

"Yes! Martin stole it when he left your apartment. Of course you would have noticed it was missing."

She shook her head. "No, in truth I have not stepped back into that room since the night of sweet Peggy's death. I was not aware he had taken the box. It is a very large wooden box, you know. My assailant toyed with it for the last few minutes of the ordeal. As if he had lost interest in me…"

Tami interjected, "As if he were just killing time?"

"Yes," Ertzbeth agreed. "Precisely as if he were simply killing time. He even removed a glove with his teeth so he could manipulate the mirrors and lenses. All the while, with the other hand, he held the nail gun steady against my heart."

"He was waiting for Peggy the entire time," I said. "Forgive me for saying this, 'Beth, but you were…"

"Just a 'prop.' I was merely set dressing for the real scene to come, between Martin Van Helsing and Peggy O'Farrel, the last descendant of the Varney conspiracy." I looked into 'Beth's eyes, expecting sorrow, grief. All I saw was hate. "The arrogance of this man. To treat the Blood Countess as a tool to be used and discarded. Make no mistake, my buddy. Martin Van Helsing dies with my teeth in his throat."

Technically, illegal. Practically, who cared? She was entitled to her payback. We all were. Frankly, I wasn't as concerned about the man's arrogance as I was about his confidence.

I pulled us back to practical matters. "I still don't get it. Why steal the camera? A symbol? A souvenir? Black market?"

Tami punched me in the arm. "Don't you listen? His fingerprints were on it. I think aside from having to grab the camera, the only flaw in Martin's plan was Peggy's shotgun."

'Beth's eyes softened. "Like her great, great grandfather, gun in hand, she stood between me and the true death. I am the strong one. I, the immortal, should have protected her. And yet she, the fragile mortal child, saved me."

"I'm so sorry, 'Beth."

"Stop it. Both of you. There is no sense in crying for me yet again, now that you know my whole story. Cry for Shelly. Cry for Knobs. The love lives of Wampyr are no more precious than those of mortals. The stories just take longer to tell."

So that left three. Three who might help Van Helsing to his treasure. Three more with prices on our heads, and one, Maarten Van Helsing, who had been marked for death by his own family. Here we all were, battered, cut, heartbroken, and boxed into a police station in the middle of New Jersey. Waiting for a bunch of Dutch ninjas to pull up in a Mercedes and kick our asses. Ladies and gentlemen, The Preposterous Seven.

You know, I don't mind taking my own licks. As long as I win in the end. But don't mess with my family. This guy had crossed way too many lines. Plus, he was making me feel stupid. I really resent being made to feel stupid. Something was nagging at me. Poking me in the back of the brain saying "Hey! Stupid! This doesn't add up. It still doesn't work. You're being played!" I really hate that voice, but I know how to shut it up. Solve the mystery.

• • • • •

Van Helsing had already shown he could be bold. He'd attacked a cop's house in broad daylight. We had no reason to believe he wouldn't try an assault on a police station. His ancestors had made a business of storming castles, after all.

Todd tried to talk me into calling in the National Guard or the State Police for help, but I convinced her that would only postpone the inevitable. The Van Helsings had been in business for hundreds of years. The bounty they were looking for had been hidden for more than a century and a half. They had the patience of vampires. If we drove them off today, they'd simply come back in a year, two, years, maybe ten. However long it took for us to let down our guard. No, no State Police or National Guard. We needed to lure them in, let them think they could take us, and end it here.

Convincing the Van Helsings they could take us probably wouldn't be too difficult. After all, half the people in the station with me were convinced they could take us. Even Maarten.

"You cannot beat them, you idiot. Martin has at least two cousins with him. By now he has probably brought in more. Each of them has received the same training I have."

"Are they as good as you?"

"Of course not. I am the best, ever. I am, as the sign says, Incredible. But in case you have not noticed, I have a punctured lung. My cousin has an inexhaustible supply of weapons and ammunition, and both lungs, while you have whatever is inside this sealed concrete box. When his team is tired of watching, he can send someone out for donuts and coffee. You will have to plunder the vending machine. His team can fight at night or during the day. Your two most powerful allies will burst into flame if they step outside at any time from dawn to dusk."

The bursting into flame part bothered me the most. Ertzbeth and B were too vulnerable during the day. I wasn't as worried as I probably should have been about going toe to toe with the Van Helsings. Knobs insisted he had a plan and, well, I'm an equal opportunity worrier. It's his plan, let him worry about it. I was more concerned Martin might try to burn us out, like the stunt he arranged in D.C. A vampire can't survive in a burning building any longer than I can. If Van Helsing played that card, it would be a Hobson's Choice for Ertzbeth and B: Burn or burn. Inside or outside, your choice.

Jean got our private network running and was keeping tabs, through Interpol's I-24/7 network, on every Van Helsing operative they could find. According to Interpol, three more cousins had booked first class flights for the States in the last 24 hours. The latest would arrive in less than three hours. Jean scraped together profiles and photos, which I took in to show Maarten. I found Ertzbeth sitting with him. Maarten was telling a story about hunting his first Baobhan

Sith through the moors of Scotland when he was a boy. Ertzbeth was captivated. "Hate to interrupt the campfire tales, but do you know these guys?"

"I know of them."

"Not a tight family, huh? They're your cousins."

"We don't gather for eggnog at the holidays, so no."

"Can you tell me anything about them?"

"They are all young. Mid twenties, at best."

"I know that. I'm the one holding the profiles."

"By young I mean they also are very green. They probably went on their first missions less than ten years ago."

"That mean they've only got..."

"That's right. They only had three or four years experience, at best, before their missions were all cancelled."

"So they're not that good."

"Exactly. Each is only slightly more deadly than anyone in this building."

"You're just a big bowl of happy, you know that?"

"Just trying to keep everything in perspective, Detective."

"Well, I'll let you Ghostbusters get back to your war stories."

I found Knobs and let him know he now had six Van Helsings to deal with instead of three. "No problem."

The Noc 1 team looked around at each other, looked at Knobs and echoed the sentiment: "No problem."

Fair enough. Like I said: His plan. His worries.

But of course I was worried. The fighting wasn't the issue. I'd seen Knobs go toe-to-toe with a gigantic savage of a werewolf and literally kick his balls in. When he told me he could take on these guys, my brain told me no way, but my gut said no problemo. I'd simply been burnt by this Van Helsing bastard too badly. He had another twist waiting for us. I could feel it.

So I did what I always do. I reached for my thinking cap. "Tami, you got a few?"

"Of course, baby. Time is all I've got. What do you need?"

"A brainstorm."

We went into my office and I poured us both some coffee. "Shoot," she said.

"What does Van Helsing want?"

"Money."

"He's a merc. Go anywhere in the world and earn it."

"Reputation."

"How?"

"Being the best."

"What makes him the best?"

"Bagging the biggest trophy."

"Who's that?"

"Jefferson?"

"Too young."

"Lord B?"

"Even younger."

"Caligula."

"In a coma. Like shooting ducks in a barrel." I led the witness. "Who's the one vampire even other vampires are afraid of?"

"The Blood Countess."

"Bingo."

"OK, so he's not after reputation." Tami surprised me with that one.

"What makes you say that?"

"He had her dead in his sights. He could have destroyed her at his leisure."

"So what, then?"

"Back to money?"

"Looks like it. Varney's fortune. It's got to be."

"But that's just the problem," Tami said. "Varney's one vampire out of thousands. 'Beth said the fortune was worth "millions." Martin drives a Mercedes Roadster! That's a ninety-thousand dollar car! He flies in back-up cousins first class. No one with that kind of pull works this hard for a few million. Ertzbeth herself is probably worth more today than the whole Varney fortune. Hell, her penthouse would go for an easy mill and a half. OK, Angus, you tell me. What are the biggest motivators for murder?"

"Money, or business. Jealousy. Revenge."

"Revenge. I like revenge." I'm not crazy about those words coming out of my bride's mouth, but she was on to something.

"What's he got against Ertzbeth?"

"I don't know. But killing is his business," she said. "We know that's why he's after us. But he's ignored the profit opportunities in hunting Ertzbeth and Lord B. Jealousy? I've got nothing. Revenge is the only thing that works."

"But according to 'Beth and B, they've never met this guy. The Van Helsing grudge has been around for centuries. Why now?"

"Yep. That's the question, Handsome. And is it the Van Helsing-Varney grudge at all? Could it be something else altogether? 'Beth has made a lot of enemies. So has B."

"Why kill Riddleton, then? Or is he a distraction, like the camera?"

"Ooh. Good question." She visibly shivered. My girl loves mysteries. "But again, I got nothin'."

"Well, you've confirmed what I've been stewing on for a few days now. Something's missing. I need to figure it out before we walk into another trap."

*****

According to Jean, we had at least three more hours (including travel time from the airport) before all the Van Helsings could possibly make it to Hawthorne. That would put us at 9 AM. I called the whole team in to the briefing room for one last run-through.

"What do we expect from them? B?"

"They will keep it personal. They will try not to involve any citizens. The FBI, the European Union and Interpol have let them mostly alone since they went quiet four years ago. They will not invite a public outcry."

"Tactics? Maarten."

"Speed. Speed, speed, then more speed. They will get here, get in quickly, kill anything in their way, quickly. Create lots of smoke and noise to confuse us. They'll go after Angus, Knobs and Tami immediately. They're the easiest, quickest targets—no offense."

"Screw you," said Knobs.

"—and cash in pocket as far the Van Helsings are concerned."

"But they must know I will never pay on this contract!" B protested. "This whole exercise is absurd!"

"You still don't get it." Maarten shook his shaggy head. "We don't… excuse me. They. They don't think that way. If you don't pay, won't pay, can't pay, one of your enemies will buy the contract, and then you will owe that enemy what you used to owe the Van Helsings. Plus interest. And when you refuse to pay that enemy, he will take a contract out on YOU. And the Van Helsings will get paid twice. It may take years, but Martin will see to it that, one way or another, Lord B, you will pay."

"OK, OK." That kind of talk wasn't helping morale one bit. "What do you expect next?"

"From there it gets complicated. They dare not kill Lord B because that would void the contract on you three. Once everyone else is dead, they might still want to torture B and Ertzbeth for the Varney information. Or, they might not kill all of you," he gestured to Tami, Knobs and me, "until they have used you as leverage against Ertzbeth or Lord B."

"Leverage?" Tami asked. "You mean, like 'Beth and Peggy?"

"Yes, Tami. Exactly like the Lady Ertzbeth and Ms. O'Farrel. They know they cannot torture information out of Ertzbeth. They do not know yet how resilient Lord B is. But they know how fragile we humans are. They'll torture you in front of the others. If I had to speculate, I think they will kill Knobs and Angus, and save you as leverage."

"Not while I'm alive," I said.

"You are probably correct," said Maarten.

"Try to," said Knobs.

"Excuse me?"

"You speak perfect English," said Knobs. "learn the words 'try to.' As in 'try to kill you.' 'Try to get in here.' This game hasn't even started yet and you've already cashed in."

"Martin took me out of the game. If he can get to me, you haven't a chance."

"Maybe you're not as good as you think you are."

The smell of testosterone was starting to curl my hair. B changed the subject. "If I am a proscribed target," offered B, "then I should remain on point in any confrontation. I can provide, if nothing else, an obstacle."

I assumed Knobs would object. Especially seeing the state he was in. But once again, he surprised me. "Good idea, B. My team's behind you. We're only loaded with lead, so you're not really in the crossfire. We've got McInnes, Olanski and the rest of the force on the roof with rifles."

"They will not open fire unprovoked," said Todd.

"I understand, Chief," I said. "We'll try to do this the right way. But you know what these guys are like."

"I know. But we're not them. We have to try."

"No argument," I conceded. "'Battle not with monsters lest ye become a monster.' We wait until they've given us no other choice."

"Damn right," said Todd. "Then we let 'em have it with everything we've got."

That drew a smile from Knobs. "If they get across the parking lot, I want to draw them in tight. Get them into close quarters. Don't give them any room to throw anything."

"I have some help coming on that front," said Tami. I nodded.

"You know Lord B and I can only help if you draw them all the way inside," Ertzbeth said.

"B will take the door. Be all the obstacle he can be. 'Beth, you're our final line of defense. I want you back by the holding cells. If they get past Knobs, B and the Noc 1s, Jean and I won't be able to hold them long. I'm counting on you to do whatever it takes to get Tami away. Somehow."

"You can count on me."

• • • • •

You can only check and re-check your weapons so many times before it actually becomes dangerous. The Brothers Grim had gotten to that point. "Put your guns down and stop screwing with them," I said. "One of you is going to shoot his own foot off." I couldn't blame them, though. I expected some activity by noon at the latest. It was after five. The sun would be down in two hours. We were hungry, cranky, anxious and bored all at the same time. Franco threw some microwave meals on for everybody, then drooled through his wired-together teeth as we knocked back Hotpockets, French bread pizza and Diet Pepsi.

'How are our people on the roof?"

"Houwa on, houwa off," mumbled Franco. They were standing lookout in short shifts. "Damn hot up dere. I bwought Pepsis and watah up."

"Good man."

After we ate I went to bring a plate to Maarten. He reclined on his cot, leaning on his unpunctured ribs. A few inches away, Ertzbeth slept. "This is ridiculous. Martin has every advantage during the day. What the hell is he up to? It's already getting dusky out there."

Maarten put a finger to his lips and nodded to the sleeping Wampyr. He whispered: "I have been wracking my brain over the same question. His tactics make no sense. In an hour the Director of the Bureau of Noctural Affairs, Lord Victor Ruthven, and The Blood Countess herself will both be able to move freely. He'd be insane to give us that advantage. Of course, he doesn't really expect to spend more than a few minutes securing your building. So perhaps he feels he has plenty of time. Nonetheless, I believe he will either do something within the next few minutes or wait until tomorrow morning."

"Wellstone!" It was Todd.

"That may be our pizza," I said.

"Excuse me?" asked Maarten.

"What we've been waiting for."

"Oh."

I found Todd near the police-only entrance at the back of the station. It opened on to the officers-only parking lot, which was surrounded with a low wall of concrete Jersey dividers. Two vehicles had pulled in, and they weren't squad cars. One was a Cadillac SUV, the other a black Mercedes Roadster. Both had blackout window treatments.

"I hope they know those windows are illegal in Jersey," said Todd.

"Let 'em know. Maybe they'll be so embarrassed they surrender."

"Commander!" It was Olanski, sprinting down the hall. "There's a car out front, too. Big fancy Range Rover. Blacked out windows."

"Thanks, Maggie." I anticipated they might come from both directions. "Tell Jean to turn off their comms." No need to make it easy for them.

A few moments later, in the briefing room, Jean turned on a small but powerful cell phone jammer. Every cell phone for a two-block radius was suddenly registering 'no signal.' Assuming they had planned on using cell phones instead of radios—we do, after all, have scanners—the team on one side of the building was now effectively cut off from the other team. I stuck my head back into the holding cell corridor. "Maarten. Wake 'Beth."

Todd grabbed a bullhorn from the equipment room and headed for the rear door. "You sure, Commander?" I asked. "It's not going to do any good."

"I know. But this is how we do it. Be ready to pull my fat ass back in if I get shot."

"Um, yes ma'am."

Todd opened the rear door, stepped briskly outside and shut it behind her. She spoke into the bullhorn. "This is Commander Todd of the Hawthorne Police Department. You are trespassing on police property in illegally customized vehicles. Remove your vehicles immediately. If Martin Van Helsing is with you, you are advised to turn him over to the police, immediately. He is wanted on suspicion of murder, attempted murder, assault, conspiracy and assaulting an officer. Any attempt to protect Mr. Van Helsing will make you an accomplice after the fact."

She lowered the bullhorn. On the roof, at least four rifles were trained on the two vehicles. Most likely another two were trained on the SUV out front. We waited for an answer. About thirty seconds passed. I wondered if they were trying to coordinate by cell phone. Todd raised the bullhorn again for another try. Before she could speak, the Roadster's passenger side door opened. The long thin form of Martin Van Helsing unfolded into the dusky parking lot. He put both hands up and waved jauntily at the snipers on the roof. Standing next to his car he spoke to Todd, but addressed everybody in the building.

"Commander Todd, I'm Martin Van Helsing. I think you're looking for me? Now, while I completely respect your authority as chief of this provincial little force, I'm afraid I can't just give myself up. You see, I'm working. And my work is very important to me."

"Your line of work, Mr. Van Helsing, is illegal."

"As are so many things these day, Commander." He started to walk toward Todd.

"Stop right there." He slowed down a little.

"Or you'll have your men shoot me? For walking across a parking lot?"

"I said stop!" She pulled her sidearm, a Glock 21 just like mine. He kept walking. "Not one more step."

He stepped. She fired. As soon as I saw Todd's trigger-finger tense, I moved. Like a sprinter off the blocks—leading with my one good leg—I burst out of the back door and crossed the three-foot distance to Todd. As Martin avoided the bullet, which I knew he would, he drew two knives and threw. This time I was fast enough. I hit Todd high enough to knock her right over. It took all my weight to do it, but we both tumbled out of the way and the knives careened off the steel door behind me. I came up firing. The four snipers opened up as well. Van Helsing got the hell out of Dodge. The back door of the armored Roadster flew open and he dove in. I shoved Todd through the police entrance, followed right on her heels and slammed and locked the door behind us.

Todd wiped the gravel from her knees and elbows. She'd held onto the bullhorn. She gave it a 'where the hell did this come from?' double-take and, with exaggerated care, placed it back in the equipment cabinet where she'd found it.

"Well, Detective. We tried it my way. You're up. Are there any shotguns left?"

·····

I quickly regrouped with Knobs, Lord B, Maarten and a groggy but eager Ertzbeth. "Change of plan. I'm pretty sure there are four out back, two out front. Maybe three and three but I doubt it. Maarten, I want you and me to take the front door."

"Is that wise?" asked Maarten.

"Well yeah, I think so. Or I wouldn't have said it."

"He has a punctured lung and you have an injured leg," said Ertzbeth.

"I'm not making myself clear. We're taking the front door. The door. We're not even stepping outside. Just holding the door. Make sure the fighting stays focused in back which is where, Knobs, I want you and your team to take the fight to them just like you described it to me."

"You figured out how to draw them in tight?" asked Todd.

"No worries."

"B, you're with Knobs. Get in the middle. Be a nuisance. Kick as much ass as you can, but mostly keep Van Helsing's men from using deadly force."

"What about me?" asked Ertzbeth.

"You're in the holding cells."

"I can be of much greater use in the thick of the fighting."

"'Beth, they got Shelly by setting Knobs and me up. They're not getting Tami that way. Not while you've got her back."

"Understood."

"Lock and load, family and friends. Lock and load."

Knobs grabbed my shoulders and pulled me in for a bear hug. "Protect and serve."

"Protect and serve."

● ● ● ● ●

I chose not to jam the regular radios because I was going to need them myself. I stuck my head into the dispatch room. "Tami! Call in your buddies." Tami grabbed the microphone. "OK, boys, load 'em in!"

The response came back: "This one's for Doctor Shelly!"

Six fire and rescue vehicles screamed around the corner, sirens wailing. Two Peterbilt 30-foot hook and ladder trucks barreled into the officers' lot, followed by two paramedic wagons. With their quarter-ton steel bumpers, the hook and ladder trucks slammed into the Caddie and the Mercedes, wedging them against the Jersey barriers. Out front, two heavy-duty rescue trucks drove up on either side of the Range Rover, wedging its doors shut.

I heard Tami on the radio. "That's great, boys! Now get the hell out of there! These guys mean business!" Out front, I watched Shelly's colleagues clamber out of the cabs and sprint down the street, flipping the Range Rover the bird the whole way.

"You didn't think to tell me about this?" Maarten asked.

"I didn't know it was going to work." I tossed Maarten a shotgun and stepped outside. I climbed up onto the closer truck and checked the situation. The car was jammed tight. Crushed. Even the back hatch was wedged under the truck's wheel well. "These guys aren't going anywhere. Let's help out back." Out back, the situation wasn't quite so pat. The trucks had squeezed the two cars toward the building, just as I'd hoped. But there was no way to get alongside and seal the cars. We arrived to find all four Van Helsing cousins backed up against their own vehicles, knives and sais drawn. One even had a bo-stick with a blade on each end. He tried to give it an intimidating spin and hit his own car. Jackass. Knobs and the Brothers Grim, wearing Kevlar and Spectra ballistic armor from neck to crotch and shoulder to wrist, were lined up no more than fifteen feet away. Knobs wanted close combat. This was as close as I could give him. He was smiling. I think he was pleased.

Someone on the roof dropped a smoke bomb. I got that idea from Martin himself. Protected by the sudden shadow, Lord B strode out into the middle of the lot. I missed whatever signal they used, but all four Van Helsings attacked as one. They surged around Lord B, who did his best to slow them down. In spite of his vampire strength and speed, B's a poet, not a fighter.

The Brothers' Grim stepped right in. Knobs had ordered them to fight two on one. The cousins were too good to go mano a mano. It irked them, but they did as they were told. As I watched, time slowed down. And I'm not getting all Lord B all of a sudden. It really looked like Knobs and the Noc 1s had slipped into slow motion. All five of them dropped into low, wide defensive crouches and contained their movements to tiny, slow pulses. No elaborate kicks. No cobra combinations. They squatted there and absorbed punch after kick after slice, not giving an inch of ground, but not returning a shred of damage, either. In contrast, in the middle of the makeshift arena, Lord B flailed with all his might and speed. He barely landed a single shot, but he kept the cousins off balance. They struggled to regroup and fend off Knobs' team's inexorable advance, but every time they braced themselves, they got tagged by the vampire. The cousins had to keep moving to avoid Lord B, but Knobs had left them no where to go. Still they cut and stabbed like an eight-armed buzzsaw. For every ten punches and cuts the Van Helsings landed, the Noc 1s managed to land one. But it was usually a big one. With the exception of Reilly, man for man Knobs and the Brothers Grim outweighed the Van Helsings by about fifty pounds. That included Angela. And when they hit, they hit hard. The Van Helsings were fast. And they were precise. But they had sacrificed strength for speed. And that's what Knobs was using against them.

So far the Van Helsings were doing all the damage. Our guys were covering up and absorbing hit after hit. A red mist of Noc 1 blood tinted the gray mantle of smoke. And still they crouched and moved inexorably forward. They weren't offering any openings for throws, and were keeping their faces and vulnerable organs covered up with massive forearms. We were betting everything on the boulders outlasting the hammers. The fight Martin expected to last two minutes had already gone on for twenty. And his cousins were looking pretty ragged.

Then we heard the ripping sound.

Not like paper. Metal. Sheet metal. From the front of the building. I ran. Maarten followed. The sun had just dipped below the roofline of Main Street. We emerged from the station's main public entrance and dove immediately for the ground. We missed, by inches, getting our heads cut off by a flying Range Rover roof. It skipped twice, like a stone on water, and came to rest against the station door.

As I stood up, I looked up. There, on top of the rescue vehicle, stood a medium-sized man with a shock of red hair and a godawful Hawaiian shirt. "Riddleton!" Maarten and I both recognized him at once. He leapt down off the truck and stalked towards us. I had nothing but my shotgun, and it was loaded for human. I let him have it, anyway. It staggered him, but as I reloaded, he backhanded me and sent me tumbling across the sidewalk. I saw Maarten go after him. The Incredible One had beaten Riddleton once. But the vampire grabbed Maarten by the throat and tossed him away like an old newspaper. He didn't even stop to open the door. He pushed through and shattered it like candyglass.

I struggled to my feet and helped Maarten up. His ribs were bleeding, badly. Blood flecks bubbled over his lips with every exhalation as he gasped for air. I got him inside, but that was all I could do for him. Riddleton was heading for the holding cells. From the end of the hallway, I shot him again, and he ignored me, again. I did an instant mental inventory of every weapon on my person. Every single thing was loaded for people. My Glock. My Sig. Both loaded with lead. I ran into my office to grab a clip of silver bullets when I heard Ertzbeth scream. Not in pain. In disbelief.

"Varney!" And then nothing but crashing sounds.

No time to dig for bullets. I grabbed my baton, Xena—at least she had silver butt caps. That was something. And I ran. Inside the holding cell block, Ertzbeth and Riddleton/Varney were trying to tear each others' heads off. They threw each other around the room with such force that they dented the bars on the cells. Tami had thrown herself over Pierowski's sedated form and seemed to be scrambling to get behind him.

There's one cell at the far end of the row that we use to hold vampires. The bars are coated with garlic oil and holy water. I'd warned Ertzbeth about it when she went in to sleep earlier that day. She dug in and threw her opponent at the bars. He screamed and spasmed in pain. I used the moment to grab Tami. "No!" she screamed and kept grabbing at Pierowski's fur. I got a better grip on her left arm and dragged her out of the cell, into the hallway. In her right hand was a big patch of fur and a tangle of IV tubes. "We have to help Ertzbeth!" And she tried to pull away but I held her tight.

"Ertzbeth can take care of herself! We're surrounded!" I heard a meaty thud from the lobby. Maarten's unconscious body came crashing down the corridor toward me. I drew both the Sig and the Glock. The two Van Helsings from the Range Rover emerged at the end of the hallway. I emptied both clips. I'm sure their body armor caught some of the lead, but not enough. Not nearly enough.

Holding Tami close, I turned from the virtually headless bodies and looked outside. Reilly and Kestler were down, as was one cousin near Knobs' feet. Lord B was engaged with a second cousin. Michaelo and Boulad had a third exhausted and backed up against the Caddie. And Knobs and Martin were going hand-to-hand right in the middle. Exactly the way Knobs wanted it, I was sure.

Martin was a whirlwind. The only times I could see his feet and hands were when they collided with some part of Knobs. Knobs was still crouched. He'd thrown off his Spectra gauntlets. His hands were covered in blood. His own and, from the condition of Martin's face, his opponent's. It looked like Martin would be catching up with his cousin in the scar department. Martin landed punch after punch and kick after kick. The ground was littered with weapons, but both fought empty-handed for the moment. I could hear Martin gasping for breath all the way inside the station. Knobs' breathing was steady as a sleeping baby. Martin threw a series of left jabs, followed by two left-hand kicks, drawing Knobs' defense to his strong right side. Like magic, a steel spike appeared in Martin's hand. He stabbed straight at the left side of Knobs' head. With no way—or time—to dodge it, Knobs caught it. With the first quick movement he'd made in almost half an hour, Knobs got his hand up and caught the spike by letting it impale his hand. Knobs has really big hands. When he grabbed the spike he also enveloped most of the fist wielding it. He flexed. Martin's wrist broke. Knobs backhanded Martin in the forehead, driving four inches of steel into his brain.

Knobs turned to the other two fights. Lord B had been knocked on his ass, and he scrambled to get back up, hissing in pain, his body pierced in a half-dozen places with silver and wooden spikes. But none had come near his heart, and his opponent was gasping as badly as Martin had been. Michaelo and Boulad had their fight under control. Their opponent had about eight square feet of movement between the Caddy and two very hard places. Another moment or two and they'd have him beat. Knobs said "Stand down."

Michaelo and Boulad responded immediately, putting plenty of distance between themselves and their opponent. B balked. For a moment. "Stand down!" And he did. As the two remaining cousins caught their breaths, Knobs told his three teammates to go inside. B looked to me. I grabbed the two silver spikes and yanked them from his gut.

"Get inside and help Ertzbeth. She's fighting Varney!"

"But that is..."

"GO!" And he went. "What are you doing, Knobs?" I asked.

He didn't take his eyes off the cousins. "Making sure they don't come back."

"Knobs, these aren't the guys who killed Shelly."

"No. This isn't about Shelly. That." He pointed to the hole in Martin's head. "That was about Shelly. This is about Tami and me and you. These guys know how we beat them. I need to make sure they don't go back and train the rest of their cousins. We don't want to lose our advantage, do we?"

"No more killing?"

"I'll do my best. It's up to them."

I gave both of them my most sincere good-cop look. "Don't make him kill you." And I pulled the door closed behind me. Strange. For nearly half an hour, the fight outside had been wordless—almost silent. As soon as I closed the door, the screaming started.

I hated leaving Ertzbeth alone with this Riddleton/Varney thing, but aside from Knobs, she kicked more ass than any of us. But it wasn't good enough. This Varney was a tough motherfucker. A lot tougher than he'd played when he'd fought Maarten. As I came through the parking lot entrance, Ertzbeth crashed through the holding cell door. We both went down hard. Me a lot harder than her, actually. Through the door I could see Lord B digging his thumbs into Riddle-Varney's eye sockets. Hawaiian-shirt didn't like that at all.

"Get Lord B out of there!" Tami bellowed from the relative safety of the equipment room. "Get him out!" Ertzbeth caught on to my bride's plan a lot faster than I did. She leapt up and charged into the room again. She landed three great John Waynes across Varney's jaw—left right left—grabbed B and bolted for the hallway. As soon as they got through, I slammed the door and locked it. Varney hit it like a truck, but between B, Ertzbeth and myself, we held it closed.

"This isn't going to last long!" I yelled, over the pounding of vampire fists on steel.

"It doesn't have to!" said Tami, holding up a huge bag of Thorazine and a tangle of IV tubing. From inside the room I heard a low roar. It grew louder and louder until the whole station shook with the power of Clawfoot's screaming.

"Jesus Christ!" I grabbed the radio. "McInnes! Bring me the tranquilizer gun! Holding cells!" Ertzbeth, B, Tami and I all pushed and shoved at the tiny window for a chance to see what was happening in the holding cells. Pierowski was up, with the remains of the silver and aconite still burning through his veins. He saw Varney and lunged. Varney was fast. He avoided a swipe of claws that would have ripped his head right off. But Clawfoot has two arms. The second set of six-inch claws impaled Varney like shrimp on a fork. Vindictive bastard that he is, Varney buried his own insignificant claws into Pierowski's paw. That just pissed the Kodiak bear off. And that's never a good idea. Clawfoot tried to shake Varney off, but with their respective claws locking them together, Clawfoot only managed to smash Varney against the wall, over and over and over again. By the time

McInnes arrived with the tranquilizer gun, Varney was nothing more than shredded flesh all over the walls and floor. I fired through the window this time. Clawfoot went back to sleep.

• • • • •

Ertzbeth guided the cleanup of Varney's remains. We carefully mopped every drop, including the khaki pants and Hawaiian shirt, into a pile at the back of our vampire holding cell. We brought in the Rev to give the bars a fresh coating of holy water and blessed garlic oil. And we waited. Sure enough, Varney the resurrectionist reconstituted himself within 24 hours. But this time, he was in a secure cell doused with holy water. The first time he grabbed the bars his hands burst into flames. The Rev's good.

• • • • •

"OK, Ertzbeth, B. Tell me. Who is this guy, for real?" I demanded. "You destroyed Varney. How much more dead could he have gotten? You threw him in a volcano!"

"It appears we threw most of him into the volcano. Something survived."

"I think I can help with that," offered Jean Vidocq. "Our family has passed this story down from generation to generation. Based on your recollections, Mademoiselle Bathory. One detail has always struck me as problematic. When Varney attacked Abraham Van Helsing, the boy defended himself with knives. According to your description, the knives cut his face and chipped away pieces of his teeth. Now, if Varney was over 150 years a vampire, at the peak of his powers, as the legends tell us, could a small boy chip away at his fangs like that?"

Ertzbeth answered. "A vampire's fangs are among his strongest weapons. No, Abraham should not have been able to do that."

"Unless the teeth were rotten. Before death. They would remain weak after death, c'est vrai?"

"C'est vrai," Tami concurred. "But we went over this when we though he was Riddleton. Rotten teeth. He's a vampire with crowns. And a pierced pecker. Q.E.D. He's English. What's that got to do with Varney?"

"He's a resurrector," I said. "Is that where you're going, Jean?" He nodded. "He completely regenerated from the shards of bloody teeth you left on the mountainside."

"That's incredible," said Lord B.

"But Riddleton was a real guy! How did Varney take his place?"

"After his resurrection he had no more access to his bank accounts and buried wealth," said Ertzbeth. "Lord B and I had hidden it all from him. He was homeless and destitute. He must have done what so many ghouls do—he followed the armies and preyed on the injured."

"If Riddleton was truly injured at Kandahar, as his military history says," said Lord B, "Varney must have finished him off and taken his place. He could have joined the Old Guard and no one in authority would ever question how Riddleton survived his wounds and came to look so very different from the veteran soldier who'd earned so many medals for valor."

"All this is very interesting," said Knobs. "But only two questions interest me: Why come after all of us, and what are we going to do with him?"

"I think Tami was right all along," I said. "It was revenge."

"But I was talking about Martin at the time."

"Think big picture, Honey. You were right. Deal with it."

"Varney had finally gotten himself to a place where he could afford to exact revenge. He wasn't about to take on the Co-Director of the Bureau of Nocturnal Affairs and the Blood Countess—sorry, 'Beth."

"Stop apologizing! I am really quite well adjusted..."

"All by himself. So who did he know who might be able to pull it off? The same guys who helped put a stop to him in 1846. And this way he got to pit two enemies against each other. No matter who won, one of his enemies would be destroyed, the others damaged badly enough that he could sweep in and finish the job. He couldn't lose."

"But he did," said Lord B.

"See, he fucked up," said Tami.

"How?" asked Knobs.

"He pissed us off."

Knobs gave a little grunt. "Huh. Damn right he did."

"Brother, I'm sorry..." I didn't have any more words.

"No, Tami's right. Letting Martin hurt Shelly was his biggest mistake. That's when we all knew this was for keeps. Now Martin's dead, which is good. But what do we do with Varney?"

"He's persona non grata, of course," offered B. "He's invisible to the law. Whatever we do, we do on our own. There will be no repercussions."

"Trust me, B," I said, "I wasn't having ethical issues with doing him in. Just practical ones. I don't want him coming back. Ever."

We thought about it. We debated it. And finally, we solved it.

• • • • •

Our trouble with Varney the Vampire had begun with old secrets and it ended with new ones. We all swore, on the blood we'd spilt that day, never to reveal the secret of Varney's fortune.

Or the tactics we used to beat the Van Helsings.

Or to tell Clawfoot Pierowski about his last big meal before the aconite worked its way out of his system.

Epilogue

We said goodbye to Shelly at the graveside at dawn. Her family's idea. Our girl was never much of a churchgoer. And hundreds of people turned out for the service, so it's just as well we didn't try to cram them all into a chapel.

Her dad spoke about his beautiful, smart, generous daughter. About her choice to forgo med school and a private practice to serve the community. About her love for adventure. He didn't mention Knobs. Or look at him. Her Mom got up and filled in the blanks. How tough it was to see her daughter in danger. But how important Knobs had been to her. How good he'd been to her. What a wonderful family they would have made.

Throughout the service Tami quietly wept. I kind of did, too. Ertzbeth and B listened from a blacked out limo by the side of the road. Todd would have been pissed. Knobs was tense, and kept looking around as if expecting some kind of attack.

Finally, as Rev said some words — lovely, I'm sure — about eternal rest and rewards, Knobs spun away so hard he nearly knocked me over. He sprinted to the back of the crowd. Straining to see over the assembled mourners, I saw Knobs hug a man in a trench coat.

He cleared back. It was Applebaum. Dr. Applebaum from Valley Hospital. The doctor handed Knobs a tiny package. Knobs pulled him close and hugged him again, then turned and worked his way back through the crowd.

Knobs returned to his seat with an altogether inappropriate grin. "Couldn't let anyone know," he said. "Not until Van Helsing was in a box." Then I saw what he was holding. Wrapped in a little pink blanket, the size of Knobs' hand, squirmed a tiny white puppy with piercing ice-blue eyes.

The author keeps the lights on as an award-winning marketing creative director.
He also sings and plays percussion for the Crimson Pirates, creates rustic pewter jewelry, and performs and directs improv comedy (often at the New York Renaissance Faire). He lives with Kelly, his bride and joy, along with a houseful of cats.

The first book of *The Overnight*,
The Law is my Shepherd, is also available.
For info, go to **donkilcoyne.com**.

Made in the USA
Charleston, SC
23 January 2013